Praise for Russ

Fifty-Six Counties: A Montana Journey:

"*Fifty-Six Counties,* a book I read with pleasure and admiration, is a great companion for those who already love Montana and for those anxious to get a real sense of the place without the salesmanship."

– Tom McGuane, author of *Gallatin Canyon*

"*Fifty-Six Counties* is animated by the numinous even as it humbles us, makes us more sane, and draws us into a new and invigorating experience of the essence of life. This is a book for Montana, for the nation, and for the world."

– Shann Ray, author of *American Masculine* and *American Copper*

"I can't wait for others to discover this book. In a voice all his own, Rowland proves to be warm and personable, and yet cutting and real—basically, one couldn't wish for a better guide to the state of Montana. This book is utterly unique. A gorgeous accomplishment."

– Laura Pritchett, author of *Stars Go Blue*

"Everything about Montana is big: its proverbial sky, its mountains, its wide open spaces. And yet, Russell Rowland has managed to capture all that grand landscape--and the people who inhabit it--into the intimacy of a single book. *Fifty-Six Counties* is a remarkable book: a macro-focused narrative using a wide-angle lens. If you have room for only one book about Montana on your shelf, make it this one."

– David Abrams, author of *Fobbit*

In Open Spaces:

Charged with dramatic tension -- a joy to read.

– Ha Jin, author of *Waiting*, winner of the National Book Award

[An] outstanding debut...Rowland's examination of family dynamics is poignant and revealing....

– *Publishers Weekly* (starred review)

"A family epic that has a muted elegance....A gracefully understated novel."
– *New York Times Book Review*

"*In Open Spaces* is sage, humane, and immensely readable."
– C. Michael Curtis, senior editor, *The Atlantic Monthly*

"A heartfelt debut...[An] unpretentious, involving story told with unfaltering authority."
– *Kirkus Reviews*

High and Inside:

"Richly and intimately told, *High and Inside* is a raucous tragicomedy, infused with the desire we all feel in the face of our greatest mistakes: to somehow win redemption, no matter how large our flaws."

– Kim Barnes, author of *In the Kingdom of Men*

"At times funny, at times tragic, often wise and always moving, this wonderful novel is a grand slam of indelible characters and infectious drama, and a flat-out great read."

– Alan Heathcock, author of *Volt*

THE WATERSHED YEARS

A Novel

by

Russell Rowland

Author of *In Open Spaces*

Fifty-Six Counties: A Montana Journey

and *High and Inside*

The Watershed Years

Published by Sweetgrass Books, Helena, Montana

ISBN 13: 978-1-59152-195-2

Printed in the United States of America

Cover design and author photo by Allen Morris Jones

Cover photo by Z.Z. Wei (http://zzweiart.com)

Text design by the author

Cataloging-in-Publication data is on file at the Library of Congress

Sweetgrass Books
PO Box 5630
Helena, MT 59604

rowlandrussell@gmail.com

This book is dedicated to Lee Arbuckle,

my godfather and favorite uncle

Watershed:

1. A ridge of high land dividing two areas that are drained by different river systems.
2. A critical point that marks a division or a change of course; a turning point

Prologue

The rain in Carter County, our little corner of Montana, rarely comes in a drizzle. Instead the sky opens and the clouds empty, accompanied by brilliant orange flashes and chest-rattling thunder.

On a spring day in 1948 I pounded staples into a twisted fence post. After spending most of the afternoon bent over, I figured I had about a half hour left before the fence would be mended. I didn't see the clouds forming. The next thing I knew, I was standing under a waterfall. Because it had been clear that morning, I didn't have my jacket with me. My shirt soaked through to my ribs, and I made a dash for the barn, running with one elbow over my nose to keep from drowning. In those five minutes, the dusty brown soil transformed into a slab of black oily gumbo. Ten feet from the barn, the mud threw my boots up over my head, and I landed flat on my back.

I scrambled to my feet and slipped into the barn. Like a swamp creature, I walked with bowed-legs, sheaths of gumbo and grass dangling from my arms. I heard talking to my left, and I started toward the sound, and almost called out. But something about the tone of the conversation made me stop. A shout echoed, and I recognized the voice of my sister-in-law Helen.

"Coward!"

I stood frozen, listening to the rain drum against the tin roof. And then I heard a thump, and my curiosity pushed me toward the sound. I heard another thump, and I saw movement in the very last stall. I hid behind the center post and watched as Helen pounded on my brother Bob with a pitchfork handle, bringing it high above her head, then down on his back time and again. I almost shouted, but a combination of curiosity and discretion told my tongue to lie still. As familiar as I was with Helen's brittle personality, I had never seen this kind of violence from her. But even more disturbing was the response from Bob. Because there wasn't one. Not only did he not fight back, but he made no move to defend himself. He sat on a milking stool like a man deep in thought, his hands resting like sleeping puppies between his knees. He took every blow.

Helen must have hit him twenty times, and the only bit of comfort I could conjure up was that Helen was too small to do much damage. She finally stopped, and tossed the handle to one side. And then she fell against Bob, as if the beating had taken every bit of her strength. She lay her head on top of his, and I watched his hand move to her shoulder, where it came to rest. And before I snuck off to the other end of the barn, where I waited in quiet torment for the next hour until the storm subsided, I heard one last sentence from Helen.

"We have got to do something."

Chapter 1

The Little Missouri Lutheran Church fluttered in the dry summer heat. Inside, a modest gathering filled the first three pews. The women wore their best hats, fanning themselves with gloves or handkerchiefs. The men sat stiff and damp in tight black suits, their bleached foreheads glistening.

I stood at the altar, hands folded, and the heat squeezed me like a rag, wringing the moisture directly from my body to my clothes. Next to me, proud and seemingly unaffected by the heat, my nephew Teddy beamed in the suit that had once belonged to his brother George. And opposite us, radiant in a pink satin dress, my sister Muriel had not stopped smiling for three days.

Pastor Ludke, now close to eighty, nodded to Gertie Snodgras, who leaned into the keyboard, coaxing the opening strains of "The Wedding March" from the pipe organ. Rita appeared at the front of the church, accompanied by my father. Rita's family, who lived in New Jersey, had sent their best wishes, but they had not come to visit Rita since my brother Jack brought her to Montana after the first war. Almost thirty years later, she hadn't been back to New Jersey either.

Jack disappeared from the ranch and from our lives in the fall of 1946, after we fished his son George's body from the reservoir. And I mean right after we found him. He disappeared directly from the scene, without a word to anyone.

Coming up the aisle, Rita smiled, dropping her eyes to the floor every other step. When she arrived in 1918, her complexion was milky white, with a sprinkling of freckles across her nose and cheeks. But Rita loved horses, and working outdoors, and she now sported the brown, weathered hide of a rancher. Her full figure complimented the simple white gown she had sewn for the occasion.

As I watched my bride-to-be sidle up the aisle, I felt her eyes take me in just as they had the first time I met her, on the train platform in Belle Fourche. I said a quiet thank you for the slow, subtle transition in our relationship.

By the time Rita reached me, I lost interest in protocol, reaching out to take her hand. Our callused palms gripped, then released, and we stood with huge smiles, side by side, facing the venerable Pastor Ludke. I thought back to the day when I was fifteen and we buried my brother and sister on the same day. On that occasion, a seemingly ancient Pastor Ludke had been at a loss to provide much in the way of comfort. He had found his voice since that day, providing support to so many families through two wars and the Depression. He now stood before us and conducted a short but heartfelt service.

Rita and I shared a shy kiss and it took me back to our first, six months earlier, when I'd come home at noon and couldn't find her. After a quick search around the house, I spotted Rita out by the chicken coop, sitting on the ground. I saw that she was crying and I approached cautiously. When I asked what was wrong, she shook her head and said simply, "My baby." I held her for a while. As we started back toward the house, my arm still draped around her waist, she looked up at me and I knew from her expression that something had shifted. I knew that if I didn't kiss her right then, I could very well disrupt the course of history.

Now Rita and I strolled down the aisle, husband and wife. But halfway, I felt a sudden stab in my forearm, the penetration of Rita's fingernails. I turned, hiding my confusion behind a forced smile. She tilted her head slightly. Her smile was also forced. When I glanced in the direction she indicated, hiding my feelings became even more of a challenge. My brother Bob and his wife Helen, who were not invited, sat right on the aisle, four rows from the front.

Worst of all, I could tell from her self-satisfied smile that Helen knew that she had already disrupted our marriage. I nodded, my smile a complete mask, and tried to convince myself that I shouldn't worry.

Because it was such a gorgeous day, we had tables set up right out in the open for the reception. The Montana prairie sang its praises to this union with a symphony of spring greens—every shade imaginable blended together. While the thick, fluttering cottonwood trees provided a solid bass line, the rich hues of our wheat sang a glorious melody. Lush fields of alfalfa chimed in with their own unique baritone harmony and the wispy heads of our budding prairie grasses fluttered above it all in a clear soprano. The grass that had originally attracted the cattle drives from Texas, the grass that had produced fat, healthy cattle for years, was back. And it was the exact same color as money.

Ever since May 19, 1937, when the Depression officially broke in Carter County with a three-day shower, we had enjoyed a steady progression of good moisture, with few signs of drought. Things were good. And thanks in large part to the dirt work that Jack had done before he disappeared, the Arbuckle Ranch was doing better than most. We had irrigation.

It had been almost fifty years since Dad filed his original homestead, and he'd worked as a cowboy for many years before, so he was tired, too tired to give much thought to the business end of the ranch. Mom had always done that. Now that she was gone and I took on more of the management duties, I came to appreciate my teachers. My father had proven to be a genius at reading the land; he knew the livestock better than he knew his own children. On the other side, my mother had shown a gift for marking trends in weather as well as market prices. Between them they made a formidable team when it came to deciding when to expand or how to recover from setbacks. I had studied their methods enough to feel confident taking on these responsibilities. The results were evident. And now we stood in the middle of that abundance, celebrating a new life. A new life that was somehow very much like the old one.

The neighbors had outdone themselves in preparation for our special day, filling table after table with shepherd's pies, salads, and casseroles of every shape and variety. One table groaned with platters of fried chicken, lamb chops, and thick cuts of beef. The wedding cake was modest, but there was no shortage of sugar. Countless pies and plates of cookies surrounded the cake like blood relatives.

We cut the cake and Rita tossed her bouquet, which bounded off someone's hands right into the lap of Margie Glasser, Steve and Jenny's daughter. Margie was sitting off to one side, not even pretending to try and catch the prize. She plucked the bundle from her lap and flung it to the side as if it was on fire. Then she blushed plum-red as the crowd erupted in laughter.

Rita and I stood in front of the dessert table and greeted our friends one by one. We smiled through comments like 'What took you so long?' and 'It's about time,' rolling our eyes in our private moments. Bob and Helen avoided the reception line, and as everyone piled their plates with food and found a comfortable place to indulge, the predictable migration occurred, with Bob and Helen's allies gathering in the far corner of the grounds.

We sat at the head table, and Dad tottered over to the chair next to mine. Decades of pitching hay, falling off horses, digging post holes, and wrestling with stubborn livestock had taken their toll on my father's back. Some days he wasn't able to roll off the mattress in the morning. He wouldn't see a doctor. Those days were hell on everyone, because he didn't want us to bother him, but he couldn't do anything on his own.

"How you feeling, Dad?" The question came to my head innocently enough, but the minute the words came out of my mouth, I regretted it.

"I'm fine," he snapped and the smile that had stretched his toothless mouth all afternoon turned downward. "Sick of people, though."

But Rita overheard my little goof, and chimed in. "That was such a nice service, wasn't it, Dad?"

"Yeah...well, I guess he should be able to pronounce your names after this many years."

"What do you remember about your wedding day, Dad?" Rita asked.

Dad had just taken a big bite of chicken. As he chewed, his chin rising nearly to the tip of his nose, a slight smile curled his lips. A thin stream of grease trickled from one side. At the same time, his eyes glistened. He blinked, then wiped his eyes, then his mouth, with the back of his hand.

"Well," he said. "Blake's mother looked like a goddam angel." He quickly took another bite, chewing his way through the emotion, his face turned down. It had been almost ten years since my mother passed, but his eyes reflected the same pain they did the day I found her tilted against the milk cow. "That red hair of hers floated out from her head like a halo."

"She always looked so nice in white," Rita said.

This was true, although I couldn't remember seeing her in white very often. It simply wasn't practical in a place where every single day required some kind of physical labor.

"God, this is good," Rita muttered through a mouthful of food.

I leaned toward her. "Which one?"

Rita pointed with her fork. "This casserole here—the one with the chicken and sweet potatoes."

"Mm, I didn't see that one."

"Here, take some of mine." Rita grabbed her spoon and started to scoop from her plate.

"No, no. I'll get some."

"Come on, Blake. Just take some. I'll get more."

"It's okay." I stood to make my way to the food table.

"Stop fighting, you two. The ink isn't even dry yet," Dad grumbled.

"Ha!" Across the table from my father, my sister Muriel's husband Stan Grant emitted one of his bursts of laughter, which always brought a smile to my face. Stan worked at the Amalgamated Copper Mine in Butte. He and Muriel had been married for many years now, with three kids.

"How are you guys doing over there?" I asked them.

"I'm just wondering when they're going to serve the main course," Stan said. "I'm getting hungry."

Muriel slapped Stan's upper arm.

"Anyone want anything else while I'm up?" I asked.

"Bring me a new set of teeth," Dad said, holding his hand to his jaw.

"You got it."

I wandered through the crowd, a big smile on my face. Several people interrupted my progress with their congratulations and smart aleck comments about how fat I've gotten since I got married. As I scooped some casserole onto my plate, I looked up to see Helen standing right next to me. I was always amazed how small she was. Barely more than five feet tall, she had always somehow managed to generate a much bigger presence.

"Well, hello, Mr. Groom," she said.

"How you doin', Helen?"

"Not too bad, considering," she said.

"Considering?" I asked, not wanting to know.

Helen placed a hand to her stomach, tilting her head toward me, smiling sideways, her apple cheeks shining.

"Oh really?" I said. "I didn't know." I tried to think of how many times she'd made this announcement, only to suffer another miscarriage.

"It's true," she said.

"Well congratulations." I shook her hand.

"And to you," she said. "You know I admire Rita very much, despite what you might think."

"I would never doubt anything that comes out of your mouth, Helen," I said.

She chuckled. "Oh, Blake, you really are the worst liar in the county…you know that, don't you?"

I smiled. "I'm going to take that as a compliment."

"As you should." She bowed her head toward me. Our eyes locked, and I felt a familiar, odd agreement pass between us—the silent admission that we would always have a begrudging respect for each other, no matter what.

"Have a good time today, okay?" I told her.

"Oh, I'm pretty sure that's your job," Helen answered, and then she turned with a sly smile.

When I got back to the table, I could see from Rita's pursed lips that she had seen the exchange.

"She's amazing," I said.

"How so?"

I just shook my head and Rita lowered her chin and her brow. She peered at me from beneath this visor. A slight grin came to her face, and I could see that she had decided that nothing was worth getting worked up about. Not today.

Sitting just on the other side of Dad was my nephew Teddy, who was now my stepson.

"You getting enough to eat there, Teddy?" I asked.

A shock of straight, straw-colored hair dangled down from the front of his scalp, tickling his eyebrows, threatening to cover his eyes. He looked up and flashed an exaggerated smile. Then he grabbed his belly, which was flat as Carter County.

Teddy had gone to work for Steve Glasser after Steve's father died. Steve needed the help, but there was another, more adorable attraction to the arrangement. Steve's daughter Margie. She of the captured bouquet.

"Teddy, do you have anything on that plate besides meat?" his mother inquired.

Teddy held up a chunk of bread.

"What about these wonderful vegetables?" Rita asked. "There's some very good corn on the cob over there, and Betty made that green bean dish you always liked."

Teddy and Dad tilted their heads toward each other and rolled their eyes.

"You want to come over here and make sure I washed behind my ears, too, Ma?" Teddy asked.

"Maybe I should," Rita said.

"Where did that expression come from, anyway?" Teddy asked. "Grandpa, did your generation have some kind of deadly behind-the-ear disease or something?"

"Back in my day, most of us were born without ears," Dad mumbled. "If you were lucky, you got a pair a hand-me-downs. I got this set from one of the Walters boys when I was twelve."

In the midst of our laughter, I noticed Tommy Strode, who was about five, staring up at my father, who had pretty big ears. I could just imagine Tommy trying to picture my father with those same ears as a twelve-year-old. Dad also noticed and he got to laughing, and couldn't stop. He'd just taken a bite of food, so he started coughing. Teddy pounded his back.

"Should I let him die, Mom?" Teddy asked.

"Teddy!" Rita squealed. "How awful. How can you say such a thing?"

"Damn kid, can't wait to get into my pockets," Dad coughed.

Teddy leaned closer to Dad, peering at his head. "Did you wash behind your ears this morning, Grandpa?"

Rita left her chair and started beating on Teddy's back. "You better behave, young man. This is my wedding day, and I'm not going to let some brat spoil it for me."

Teddy covered his head with both hands and started screaming. "Somebody help me. This woman's gone crazy. She's lost her head!"

If there had been anyone who wasn't paying attention, they were now. The crowd gathered around and cheered for Rita, or pleaded mercy for poor Teddy. I stood up and made a dramatic show of approaching my new wife with a threatening glare. I broadened my shoulders and bowed my arms. The crowd noise got louder. I picked up a big wooden spoon and started smacking it against my palm as I came up behind Rita.

"Show her who's boss!" somebody yelled.

"Woman!" I shouted.

Rita turned around and played right into the scene. She covered her face with her hands and started to run away in tiny steps, screaming in a high-pitched voice. I chased her with a bear-like lumber, holding the spoon above my head like a club. Rita trotted around the yard, with me in hot pursuit, the procession following, shouting encouragement or jeering. The shouting and laughter were so loud that it took a while to notice a single, piercing scream from the other side of the grounds.

The realization passed slowly from person to person, with small clumps drifting toward the opposite corner, drawing the attention of a few more. The noise dwindled and soon we were all aware that something was wrong.

The scream subsided for a moment, but when it resumed, I recognized Helen's voice. We all ran over to the cluster of people and I squeezed through. Helen was lying on her back, holding her abdomen.

As hard as I had tried to despise this woman through the years, I also knew that if there was one thing she wanted more than anything in the world, it was a child. I pushed through to the front, leaning over my brother.

"Let's get her to the doctor, Bob."

Bob looked up at me, a combination of fear and sadness twisting his brow. "She doesn't want to go, Blake."

I suddenly felt a presence close to my elbow. "Hell, she's faking it." Dad peered down at Helen and I watched a look of furious indignation come into her eyes.

"Dad, don't say that," Rita said.

Bob pulled my father away from his wife, and I heard him mumble, "That was a cruel thing to say, Dad."

"Yeah, well, maybe you'll think about what you've gotten yourself into for once," Dad said.

Squatting next to Helen, I was amazed to see her intently watching this exchange.

"We need to get you to the hospital," I said.

She shook her head, and although her face twisted in pain, she said, "I don't want to spoil your day, Blake."

Rita appeared at my side and I squeezed her hand. "It's going to take a lot more than this to spoil our day."

"Helen, do you want us to take you somewhere more discrete?" Rita asked.

Helen nodded, and as Bob and another man crouched and lifted her, Helen did not take her eyes off my father. Even as they carried her into the church, she continued to glare at him.

Chapter 2

Exactly one week after my wedding, I waded out into the early morning dew, shading my eyes from a semicircle of sun. A voice from behind and to my right startled me.

"Excuse me," I heard.

I turned to find a man no taller than a pony.

"Mornin'," he said.

"How you doin'?"

"Good...good. Name's MacArthur." He offered his hand, which was as hard as a stone. I told him my name, and although we shook for only a second, I could feel his strength all the way up my arm. His body looked like a series of fists, muscles bunched and piled up on top of each other, testing every seam in his sky blue western shirt. Even his head sat on his shoulders like the largest, most imposing fist of all. His hair was a red stubble and he peered up at me through the cloudy lenses of wire-rimmed spectacles that magnified his blue eyes.

"I guess you're looking for work?"

"That's right." His smile was warm, inviting. I also noticed, behind the murky lenses, that the whites of his eyes were clear, like egg shells. He was a bit older than most of the men who showed up at our door, though probably still in his twenties.

There were several other things that were unusual about this introduction. First, a man who was looking for work in our parts rarely showed up at 5:00 in the morning. And second, if he did show up at 5:00 in the morning, there was a good chance he was either still drunk or very hung over. And third, Mr. MacArthur had shaved. He didn't have a hint of red whisker on his chin.

"Where you comin' from?" I asked.

"Well, I've been working for a man near Belle...Tabor." He had been twisting a gray felt cowboy hat in his tight fists and he now tugged it onto his head.

"And?"

"Well, I worked there for several years, and that situation has just run its course, you might say."

My respect for this little man increased tenfold with this statement. I knew Garland Tabor from REA meetings and he was one of the more difficult men I'd ever met.

"Walk with me," I said. "I need to get my milking done."

"You can't get your wife to do the milking for you?"

I chuckled. "Funny you should ask. I just got married a week ago, and I offered to milk the cow for the first month we're married. A little wedding gift, you might say."

"And you don't regret that offer?"

"Every morning at five."

After a short laugh, he offered his congratulations.

"Thank you. What's your first name, MacArthur?"

"Oscar."

"Really?"

"Yep. My German mother."

"Ah. Okay. Scottish dad?"

"As tight as they come," he said.

"Well, you'll fit right in here. I'm Scottish myself," I said.

"I thought Arbuckle might be one and the same," he said in a perfect Scottish brogue.

For the rest of the walk to the barn and the time it took to milk the cow, I asked Oscar MacArthur the standard questions I'd ask any prospective hand. But it was just a formality as I knew from that first handshake that this man had a job.

Although most of the ranches had become more efficient since the war thanks to improved machinery, they had also gotten bigger with so many people leaving in the thirties. Those of us who stayed acquired land in chunks. There was a lot of work to do. The bigger ranches needed haying crews, harvest crews, and shearing crews. There were men who organized these crews, moving from place to place, earning most of their money during those seasons. Then there were the sheepherders. But that was a solitary life, more suited for older, often eccentric men who were comfortable being alone for weeks at a time.

If a young man was a good, steady worker, his ideal position was to hire on as a year-round hand for one of the bigger ranches. Ever since the war ended, young men had been flocking to our door, sporting a three-day stubble and carrying a satchel filled with work clothes. Many of these men were fractured somehow, if not by the war, then by a lost love or the loss of their own family place. They were generally hard on the outside but tender souls, unable to shake off a harsh word.

The pattern was often predictable. After working like their lives were at stake for the first few weeks, something would rub them the wrong way, and their productivity would drop in small but steady increments. Then they would disappear for three or four days and come back with the battle scars of a bender. We always asked them to leave after these episodes. There were other places that were more forgiving. But with so many prospects, we didn't need to tolerate unreliability.

There were also a fair number of shady characters who showed up with remarkably bad haircuts and shaky references. We usually turned away the boys who were obviously just out of jail. But occasionally, a hand would take a few 'gifts' when they disappeared—maybe a rifle, or a saddle.

We fell victim to thieves only a couple of times for one simple but mysterious reason. Despite spending less time around people than almost anyone I knew, my father possessed an amazing knack for spotting a man with a nose for merchandise. Countless times, I watched my father talk to a man who said all the right things, bore calluses in all the right places, and had all the right gear. Dad would never look a man in the eye when he questioned him, but he drew a conclusion, and on those occasions when he told someone, "Well, you seem like a good hand, but we don't really need anyone right now," I'd learned to keep my mouth shut. Sure enough, there had been at least five instances where word came back that these men were thieves. One even stole a horse.

I asked Dad about it once. "All you gotta do is listen to their voice. If they got something to hide, they sound like they got something to hide."

I tried to figure out what he meant by this, but I could never hear it. I apparently didn't inherit that particular ear.

"What about you, Oscar? No family?"

"I had a wife," he said without hesitation. "Didn't make it through the Depression."

"Sorry to hear that."

"Took her own life," he offered, an unusual confession to someone he barely knew, I thought. I didn't know what to say.

"It was a horrible thing to do," he continued. "Tore up everyone who ever loved the poor girl."

Again, I was speechless. But I managed a nod.

"Not that I hold it against her," Oscar said. "I really can't blame her at all. From the time I met Sadie, there was something dark and powerful working away at her. Something a hell of a lot more powerful than her—or me. There wasn't anything anybody could do to make that poor girl see the good in the world."

"That's tragic," I muttered.

"It is." Oscar stopped. "It is tragic. Because the world is a beautiful damn place."

"Yes it is." I was embarrassed by this sentiment, and couldn't look at Oscar. I kept my focus on the milking.

"I got a proposition for you," Oscar said.

"Let's hear it."

"How 'bout I milk that cow for you and we won't tell the missus." MacArthur jerked a gnarled thumb toward the barn.

If I hadn't already been taken in by this man, his method of asking for a job certainly would have done the trick. "Well now, Mr. Oscar MacArthur, I just might be interested in that proposition, but how much is that little deal gonna cost me?"

"How about six dollars a day?"

"How about four dollars a day?"

"How about six dollars a day?"

I laughed. "What the hell kind of negotiation is that?"

"Oh, are we negotiating?" He smiled, and his blue eyes twinkled behind those thick lenses.

"You got a horse?"

"Oh, do I have a horse..." Oscar pointed toward the house, but the horse wasn't in view. "Patsy is more than just a horse. She's a legend."

I smiled. "Okay. Six it is."

We shook, and I swear, my hand hurt for the next four hours.

Oscar went off to take Patsy to the barn and get her fed and watered, promising to finish the millking when he had her settled in. When I came back to the house and sat down at the table, Rita took one look at me and asked, "What are you smiling about?"

"Was I smiling?"

She set a plate of eggs, bacon and fried potatoes in front of me. "Like a circus clown."

"I think I just hired the best hand in the county."

An hour later, in the barn, I was saddling my horse alongside Oscar when Dad came limping in.

"Dad, this is Oscar."

"Howdy." Oscar reached for Dad's hand, and I flinched when he took it, thinking of Dad's arthritic joints cracking in Oscar's grip. Dad didn't show any sign of pain, but of course he wouldn't, even if his hand turned to powder.

"Dad, you want to work on that line of fence along the Big Meadow while Oscar and I move those heifers?"

"No, I'll ride along with you boys. We probably need three of us to get 'em through that draw along Hay Creek."

I thought about how long I'd been trying to get the sloping length of fence mended, but I didn't argue. It had become obvious in recent months that he preferred to be around other people.

By this time we had fallen into a comfortable routine at the Arbuckle Ranch. Bob was an expert with the machinery, so he had taken charge of the farming. Each morning he parked himself on the old tractor and mowed, plowed, planted or furrowed. Dad and I handled the stock, which meant that the only times the three of us worked together were harvest, branding, calving and lambing.

But my father was in his seventies now. And although nobody would have thought less of him for taking it easy, he was like most men of his generation—driven by fear. Fear that failure was imminent. That the next dry month would destroy everything he'd worked for. It was a reasonable fear, because we'd seen it happen so many times. But his joints were worn down. A couple of his ribs had separated from his spine, which brought a pain that sometimes threw him to his knees. None of this mattered. He needed to be out there as much as most of us need to fill our bellies with food.

"God damn, it's a beautiful day!" Oscar tipped his hat as far back on his head as he could and lifted his face to the sun.

I looked around as if to verify this. The grass was thicker than it had ever been and as green as a fresh-cooked bean. It even smelled sweet.

Dad rode up alongside Oscar, and I could tell by his quizzical look that he wasn't sure what to make of him. "Where you from, Oscar?"

"Grew up in Idaho, near Boise. Lost my folks pretty early on, but I had a bunch of relatives that took turns warming my butt. Good people. Loved to fight, though. Yelling all the time, my family."

I saw Dad's mouth curl into a slight smile. "Only child?"

Oscar nodded. "Yes I am. Lost a baby sister when she was just a couple years old."

I thought about the bodies piling up in Oscar's past. He'd suffered more loss in his short life than anyone deserved.

"How'd you end up here?" I asked.

"Rodeoing." Oscar lifted a leather rope that was laced to his saddle. The leather looked like old copper, it was worn so smooth and shiny. "I was a calf roper. Did the circuit for a while, but I couldn't make enough money to live on. Ran out of money just after the roundup in Belle, and took the job with Tabor."

"You worked for Tabor?" Dad asked.

"For several years."

Dad raised his brow. "And you didn't kill the SOB?"

Oscar smiled, taking off his glasses and rubbing them against his shirt. "He's not so bad. He's got a temper, but once you figure out what sets him off, you just learn where to hide when you see it coming."

After watching Dad ignore most of our hands for the last several years, it was nice to see him press for more details. It turned out Oscar had also won several horseshoe tournaments around South Dakota and Montana. He shared his accomplishments in the same matter-of-fact tone that he'd talked about the deaths of his family.

The sun climbed upward, and we swigged from jugs of warm water, and wrapped damp kerchiefs around our necks. We reached the far end of the Hay Creek Pasture, where we surrounded our cud-chewing cattle and coaxed them into a herd. We then pushed them along the fence-line toward the gate.

I watched Oscar work his horse, Patsy, and with his rodeo background, it was no surprise that he was a magical horseman. He reined the pony with easy, calm movements, almost as if he was talking to her with his hands. The horse had the same calm demeanor, sometimes even appearing to nod when Oscar nudged her in a certain direction, as if to say, 'Yeah, I was just about to suggest we head over that way.'

When I wasn't mesmerized by Oscar MacArthur's horsemanship or trying to redirect a rebellious Hereford, I stole an occasional glance in Dad's direction to make sure he wasn't pushing himself too hard. But he looked good...healthy, with a rich color, as though meeting this man who was so full of life was somehow contagious.

I was just about to suggest that we stop and break for dinner when a cow suddenly decided she'd forgotten her purse or something. She turned around and headed in the direction we'd come from, moving with a speed that only the more stubborn cows seem to possess. Oscar started after her, but Dad was closer and held up a hand. "I got her." He draped a rein across his horse Mulie's neck and she reluctantly followed his lead, fighting, knowing they were turning away from the barn.

Oscar and I plodded ahead, although I kept an eye on Dad. It seemed that we were in for a quiet afternoon. I even began to nod off as my horse Mouse settled into a steady rhythm. But a swift motion interrupted this doze, a motion I heard more than I saw. A loud creak of leather, then the whoosh of a horse turning, and hooves pounding the hard ground at a gallop. I turned to see Oscar racing toward Dad. I reined Mouse toward the scene, and when I saw what drew Oscar in that direction, I buried my boots in Mouse's flank. "Come on, girl."

Dad sat slumped in the saddle, leaning to one side, barely hanging onto the horn. Oscar reached him before I was halfway there, and he hopped off Patsy, jumping up and wrapping his arms around Dad, letting him fall into him. Oscar pulled Dad to the ground and laid him gently on his back. After feeling Dad's neck and his chest and touching a hand to his cheek, Oscar bent over and planted his mouth on Dad's. I was just arriving, and I swung to the ground, crouching next to Oscar as he breathed into my father. When he exhaled, Oscar rose up dramatically, lifted both of those rock-hard fists high above his head, and planted a punch against my father's chest that made my teeth hurt. He hit him once, twice, a third time.

"What are you doing?" I asked, but it was more of a thought that had worked its way into my throat than a real question. I didn't expect an answer, or want one, especially when Oscar went back to breathing life into my father. Watching this procedure, I was struck by the dramatic swing from violence to tenderness.

Oscar came up for air. "Get something to put under his head."

I dug into my saddlebag for my raincoat, which was rolled up. I lifted Dad's head and wedged the coat beneath it.

I then knelt at my father's head, and took a good look at his face. He was dead. There was no doubt about it. His eyes stared with a vacant emptiness I'd seen too many times in my life. His jaw hung open an inch. His skin was pale as milk. Oscar pounded his chest again.

Then he wasn't dead. A cough rattled his chest, and he blinked rapidly. His head rotated from side to side. His cheeks flushed pink. The cough continued and a short, staccato laugh escaped my throat. A sour look came over Dad. Oscar continued to press down on his chest in a steady rhythm.

"Stop that, dammit!" Dad tried to push Oscar off, but he was too weak. But Oscar did stop, placing two fingers to Dad's neck. He held them there while Dad gasped, his labored breath interrupted by an occasional cough. Without thinking, I realized I had taken Dad's hand in my own and was squeezing hell out of it.

"You okay, George?" Oscar asked.

Dad clawed at Oscar's hand, prying it from his neck. "I'm fine."

Oscar and I leaned back on our haunches. I released Dad's hand. We kept our eyes locked on his, watching as the color returned to his face and his breath came more easily. As Dad's awareness came back, so did his discomfort with the two of us staring at him.

"I'm all right," he said several times. And finally, "Let's get back to these cattle."

"Oh no you don't," I said. "You're going back to the house. Oscar, you go on in with him. I'll get these cows over to the other pasture."

Oscar nodded, but Dad said, "I'll be fine. I'm not going anywhere."

"Dad, this isn't a discussion. You need to get home."

"You just had yourself a heart attack, Mr. Arbuckle."

"That wasn't a heart attack," Dad insisted. "Just some gas. Something I ate." Dad pried an elbow under his torso and tried to lift himself, but midway he went pale again. Sweat erupted from his pores, coating his face with a slick sheen. He eased himself back onto the ground.

"Okay?" I asked.

Dad nodded, and I could see that this concession came closer to killing him than the heart attack had.

We waited a long time before moving him, getting him to drink as much water as he could. After twenty minutes, he was able to sit up. This simple act brought another flood of sweat to his brow. His breath came fast, as if his throat had closed to the width of a thread. And I saw something I'd never seen. My father's eyes widened, darting from side to side. The man was scared to death and couldn't hide it. Oscar and I lifted him up on Patsy and Oscar sat behind him, leading Mulie as they headed toward the barn.

For the next three hours, Mouse did most of the work. My mind couldn't focus on the task at hand. Mouse seemed to sense this, as she moved without direction, guiding the herd along the fence line. It was almost as if Patsy had been schooling Mouse all morning. I had just enough presence to open the gate, and the Herefords ambled through, bored with the imposition.

I was worried. I figured I probably should have gone back to the house—not because I could have done anything, but just because I should be there. The dead quiet of the Montana prairie provided little distraction, aside from shuffling hooves and the occasional, feeble complaint from a cow.

Unlike the fences that keep the stock from wandering, there is nothing out here to contain your imagination. Because of the quiet, your mind is free to travel. This is dangerous when you're afraid, or angry or unhappy. These thoughts are fed by the silence. They grow and become larger than they should be. When you feel it happening, you try and stop it. You realize it's not logical, so you try to talk yourself out of being afraid. But this just feeds it.

I rode through the Big Meadow with a fear that swelled and shifted and grumbled in my chest like a thundercloud. I was afraid of losing my father, of course. But I was also thinking about death in general. When my brother George drowned in 1916, I was only fourteen, and couldn't comprehend the possibility that death could just as easily visit me. Each death since then had chewed away at my invincibility. The fear grew, and the quiet fed it, and despite being ridiculous and illogical, I could barely breathe by the time I rode into the barn and unsaddled Mouse.

I walked briskly past Bob and Helen's house, thinking that I should probably let them know. But I was too anxious to see Dad. I entered the house, and Rita met me with her hands on her hips. "Where have you been?"

I frowned. "They didn't tell you?"

"They told me you were moving the cattle, but I couldn't believe you'd be so thoughtless."

"How's he doing?"

"He's okay. He's sleeping." She crossed her arms. Her hair was pinned on top of her head, but several dark strands had sprung loose, dropping into her face.

"Honey, you know we have to help Glassers with branding the next two days. Those cattle needed to be moved today."

Rita had started back toward the kitchen, but she stopped. "I'm sorry. I forgot all about the branding. I was just surprised you wouldn't want to be here."

"I did want to be here."

She sighed, and breathed in, nodding.

I put my arms around her.

Dad's room was dark, with the shades drawn. He was asleep. I leaned over him and peered into his face. His skin looked pasty, his thin lips almost as colorless as the rest of him. Even his tongue looked white between his teeth. In fact, his teeth, with their tobacco stains, had more color.

I sat on the mattress next to him for a few minutes. And then I heard Rita call for supper. As I began to stand, Dad's eyes opened. Just like that, he had the same wide, fearful look I'd seen that afternoon.

"Who was that guy?" he asked.

"What guy?"

"The one who saved my life."

Chapter 3

A fire blazed in the middle of the Glasser corral. Three branding iron handles emerged from the fire like toothpicks, their Rocking G molds glowing orange in the flame. Steve's Herefords milled around the corral, their copper coats reflecting the hot sun. They expressed their unhappiness in loud 'MAW's and glared at us whenever they caught our eye. Steve manned the irons. Oscar and I did the roping, and Teddy handled the gate, letting the newly branded calves free and keeping a tally by marking a plank with charcoal. This left the job of wrestling the calves to the ground to Bob, who had spent so much time on the tractor lately that he looked a little worn out. Oscar offered to take his place after dinner.

"I'm fine," Bob said.

I sometimes lost track of my job, watching Oscar rope or work with Patsy, who moved between the cattle like a dancer while Oscar flipped his rope. The loop would extend from his hand like a beam of light, with Oscar murmuring to Patsy the whole time. "That's it," he'd say. Or "Right, girl. Right." She'd nod and adjust.

I had noticed another interesting thing about Patsy. She did not like Bob at all. She'd taken a few nips at him, and anytime he came near her, she would throw her head to the side as if she couldn't stand the smell of him.

"You sure you don't want me to take over…maybe after dinner?" Oscar asked Bob.

Bob bristled. "Maybe after dinner."

"How many so far?" Steve asked Teddy.

Teddy studied the plank, touching the groups of five with his glove as he added in his head. "Fifty-nine!"

"Not bad for a morning," I said.

"Gettin' there," Steve said.

Ever since Steve's dad Gary died the year before, Steve had been a different person. Gary was a good man, but I don't think he'd ever relaxed in his life. He looked as if he was just waiting for somebody to give him the worst news imaginable. It wasn't unusual to walk into the Glasser household and feel as if you were interrupting something.

"Where's the water?" Bob asked.

"Water?" Steve asked. "What makes you think we got water?" Steve had a skewed eye, which now wandered to Bob's left.

Bob frowned. "I saw Teddy drinking some."

"I was kidding. Jesus, Bob." Steve playfully punched him in the arm. "Where's your head today?"

Bob bristled, strolling over to the water jug. I had noticed Bob's mood, too, and wondered whether he was thinking about Dad.

I nudged Mouse toward the closest calf, twirling the rope above my head. As soon as I isolated the little guy in one corner, Oscar flipped his lasso, which settled like a shadow around the calf's neck. Patsy backed up, and the rope went taut. I dropped my loop on the ground behind the calf, and Oscar let out just enough slack that the calf stepped back, right into the lasso. I flipped my rope and backed Mouse up, and the calf tipped to its side. Bob laid a knee into its ribs, and Steve approached with a hot iron.

"Must be about time for dinner, isn't it?" Bob asked.

"Pretty soon," Steve answered. He carefully positioned the rocking G against the calf's flank, and the smell of burning hair filled the air.

"You're a hell of a roper, Oscar," Steve said. "Where'd you say you found this guy, Blake?"

"I caught him stealing a chicken," I said.

Oscar laughed.

"You got any brothers?" Steve asked.

"Not that I know of," Oscar answered.

"Well, you better keep an eye on this guy, Blake. I might just have to kidnap him."

"Not without taking a bullet to the head," I said.

"That's a pretty steep price," Steve said thoughtfully.

"You guys stop talking about me like that or I'm gonna start blushing," Oscar said.

"Ouch. God damn that horse." Bob jerked his shoulder to one side, glaring at Patsy.

"All right," Steve said. "Maybe it is time for dinner."

Jenny and Margie had prepared roast beef sandwiches with potato salad and green beans. Jenny was pale, and every small task seemed to require her complete concentration. Any question that came her way threw her into a visible panic.

I'd always been baffled by Jenny's nervous condition. The only common thread among victims of 'the loneliness' was that they generally hadn't grown up on a ranch. But Jenny's folks had homesteaded just a year or two after mine, so she'd lived in this country her whole life.

On the other hand, the second common thread with 'the loneliness' was physical weakness. Watching Jenny shuffle around the Glasser kitchen, her pale skin flushed with effort, I couldn't help but compare her to Rita, with her rich tan and solid build.

"When are you guys planning to cut your hay?" Steve looked at me, although his skewed eye pointed toward Oscar, who shrugged.

"Bob?" I turned to my brother.

"Next week," Bob said.

"God, the hay's looking good this year, isn't it?" Steve said.

"I can't remember it being this thick," I agreed.

"1915," Steve said.

Everyone nodded.

"Did you hear that Christophs are trying to sell?" Steve asked.

"Are they really?" I asked.

"I just can't imagine how anyone could get through the thirties and not make a go of it now," Oscar said.

Steve tipped his head back, miming a drink from a bottle.

Teddy shook his head. "That's sad."

"Honey, could you please bring us some more butter?" Steve called into the kitchen. "Well, he's had plenty of chances."

"That's for sure," I said. "It's still sad."

Seconds later, a crash echoed from the kitchen, a plate exploding against the floor. While the rest of us barely flinched, Steve jumped to his feet, running to the kitchen.

"What is it?"

Quiet muttering followed, but Jenny's voice grew in a steady beat of increasingly angry syllables. Eventually, we heard, "It's …this…constant…"

"Come on, darling. It's okay." Steve's voice trembled with a tired effort at assurance. "Let's go lie down. Come on."

"I'm doing all I can here…I'm doing the best I can…and every time I turn around…every time I feel like I'm doing…I feel like I'm…I do everything I can…and I just…I just can't figure it out."

Steve led Jenny through the dining room, his big arm wrapped around her waist while the words continued to burst from her mouth like broken teeth.

"Sorry, folks," Steve said, but the last thing we wanted was an apology.

Jenny's face twisted into a pained frown. She completely surrendered to Steve's guidance as he led her to the bedroom, where he stayed. Margie joined us at the table now that she didn't have to keep an eye on her mother. But she ate quickly, then also retired to her parents' bedroom. The rest of us finished dinner with little to say. Although we'd all heard about Jenny's episodes for years, I'd never been present for one. And I had to wonder what it must be like living with the possibility of these outbursts hanging over the family. So much of our lives were already shaded with unpredictability. The weather, the livestock, the insects and equipment failures. All out of our control. It made Steve's attitude even more remarkable.

None of us spoke of the incident for the rest of the day. We returned to our branding without Steve, although he showed up an hour later. We greeted his apology with a chorus of, 'Don't worry about it, Steve' and 'Hell, we don't need your help anyway.'

Despite his effort to hide it, I caught a trace of moisture in his eye as he returned to his post at the branding fire. It was a time-honored code in our country, to not acknowledge or encourage this kind of show of emotion. It was too inconvenient, too distracting. There was too much that needed to be done to get caught up in matters of the heart.

Chapter 4

Late one evening Rita and I sat at the dining room table, drinking coffee and going over our finances. The numbers filled up the rows from line to line. Dad dozed in his chair in the living room, where he now spent most of his days listening to the radio. We would wake him when we were ready for bed, and he would stagger to his room.

"So how many head are you thinking about buying?" Rita asked.

"Around a hundred."

"A hundred?" She whistled.

"We can afford that."

"Yeah, we can afford it, but should we go that high? Remember, we still have to get that new thresher before harvest."

"I know." My voice got tight.

Rita sighed. After being single for over forty years, I was used to making decisions and then simply acting on them. I hadn't grown accustomed to this idea of discussing things. It always felt like a waste of time.

"I don't want to fight about this," Rita said. "So go ahead a get a hundred." She left the room and I knew we would fight about it later.

Moments after she left the room, the back door opened and Teddy slumped through the room. He didn't say hello.

"Whoa…hold your horses there." I held up one hand. "What's going on?"

Teddy stopped, but kept his back to me. "I'd rather not talk about it."

"The lovebirds get tangled up?"

"It's not a good time to joke, Blake." He started to leave the room, but I got up.

"I'm sorry, Teddy."

The sound of Teddy's voice brought Rita back into the room. "What's going on?"

Teddy sighed, dropping his head. "It's Mrs. Glasser. They had to put her away again."

"Oh no. I'm sorry, son." Rita started toward him, but Teddy raised a palm. She laid a hand on his arm anyway.

I wanted to ask what happened, but I decided to respect Teddy's request.

"What happened?" Rita asked.

Teddy shook his head. He started to say something, but his hand flew up into the air in a gesture of helplessness. And he shook his head again.

"Should we give Steve a call?" I asked.

"Maybe you ought to wait 'til tomorrow," Teddy said. "He's in pretty bad shape."

"'Course." Rita patted his upper arm.

"I'm going to sleep for a while." Teddy plodded off to his old room, and I had to wonder why he wasn't with Margie. The strain had probably been too much for the young couple.

Rita and I shared a frown. Hearing about these things never got easier, no matter how often we'd encountered such stories. Because the loneliness was like a virus, and the proximity of it served as a reminder. Even when we felt strong, prosperous…when it looked as if we would have yet another good year, we all knew the climate could change in the slightest turn of this big ol' world.

"Maybe I should just go with fifty head," I said. We exchanged a nod before going in to give Dad a nudge.

The next day, as Oscar and I headed for the barn, the sounds of metal banging on metal echoed from the shop. When we passed, Bob was working on the tractor. After a slight hesitation, I turned to Oscar and tilted my head toward the shop.

"How's it going?" I asked Bob.

"It's been better." Bob didn't look up.

"What's wrong?"

"Nothing worth talking about."

Oscar and I exchanged a look, raising our brows. "Well, we're going to town for the auction tomorrow. You need anything?"

"Nope."

A brief silence passed as I tried to think of something to prolong the conversation. But nothing came to mind. "Talk to you later." Bob didn't bother answering.

We strolled out of the shop, and as we made our way toward the barn, Oscar chuckled. "You plan on telling me what's going on with that brother of yours, or does this family never talk about that stuff?"

I chuckled. "Well, there's some truth to that…not talking. But it's a long story."

"I got all damn day."

I thought hard about whether I should share the history of Bob and Helen. It would be easy to make a case that Bob and Helen couldn't be trusted. A quick recap of how Helen rummaged through my things and found a letter years before, or the money they stole from the ranch, or her accusations of an affair. I could easily bring Oscar into our little fold as an ally. But it didn't feel right.

"Let's just say we don't exactly see things the same way."

Oscar laughed. "That's your idea of a long story?"
I could only smile. "Well, I left a few parts out."

Oscar and I strolled through the Belle Fourche auction yards, armed with a pad of paper, taking notes on various cattle. Carter County's cattle were bigger than most, as always.

The atmosphere of these Thursday stock auctions, like everything since the Depression broke, brought back memories of the early 1900s. The crowd buzzed, and cheeks shone with anticipation. In a country where we so often work alone, we relish the opportunities to congregate. Throw in the anticipation of buying new stock, and a special kind of current runs through the crowd. At the same time, our stoic nature demands that we sit with the grave expressions of spinster aunts, acting as if nothing in the entire county holds our interest.

The auctioneer kicks off each auction with his machine gun delivery, his tongue rattling, the numbers jumping out like miracles within a steady stream of staccato syllables. They release a herd of Herefords into the pen, and the cattle mill around with a nervous fear, crying for some lost sense of comfort. Being there together, with their old friends, does nothing to ease this fear, and their fight for survival becomes a solitary one. They sense something wrong, and they scan the arena, looking for some assurance. Their eyes lock into yours, and the expression asks, "How did this happen? How did I end up here?"

And we bid. We bid without fanfare, tipping our hat brim, or making a subtle flip of our program. One guy touches his eyebrow with two fingers. Another emits a shrill, brief whistle. Spotters prowl in front of the grandstand, pointing out the bidders and shouting "Hey!"

to signal to the auctioneer to bump up the number. It's a remarkable, efficient, almost perfect ballet of commerce.

Halfway through the auction, they loosed some Herefords from the Hash Knife, a ranch near Alzada that had been producing some of the best cattle in the area for decades. My dad had worked as a cowboy for the Hash Knife before he made his claim on our place, and said he'd learned most of what he knew about stock there. The crowd sat up straighter. The sweet smell of straw lingered. Even Ed Smykal, the auctioneer, paused for a moment.

"Ladies and gentlemen, who's gonna open the bid at thirty?"

Two fingers to the eyebrow started a flurry. Ed had a hard time keeping up as the spotters bayed like angry dogs, barking over each other as the bids came fast and desperate. I made a couple of early bids, but they didn't need my help raising this price. I also remembered my promise to Rita. This herd had seventy-five head.

"They're going too high," Oscar muttered.

"They sure are."

The bid rose steadily, in chunks. Sweat washed Ed Smykal's face, and Oscar and I scanned the program for other possibilities. Bidders dropped out, until it came down to two stubborn souls. While Ed's tempo remained steady, the barks of the spotters came further and further apart.

"I can't believe how high these guys are going," I whispered to Oscar. "What the hell are they thinking?"

Oscar just shook his head. I watched one of the bidders, who sat to our right and delivered his bid with a backward extension of his pointer finger. The second bidder sat behind us, also using a silent bidding method. I turned around to see who it was, but there was a couple sitting behind us that...well, let's just say they've had a few juicy steaks through the years.

Ed repeated the bid over and over, like a phonograph record with a scratch. "Seveny-five, seveny-five, seveny-five…do I hear seveny-seven….seveny-five, going once…going twice…"

"Hey!" A spotter barked.

"Seveny-seven," Ed called out, his voice rising. "We got a seveny-seven dollah bid…we got a bid of seveny-seven…do I hear eighty…do I hear eighty…we got seveny-seven, seveny-seven, seven-sevennnnnndo I hear eighty…I'm looking for a eighty dollah bid…seveny-seven, seveny-seven, going once, going twice…" Pause. "*Sold*! For seventy-seven dollars a head…to the Arbuckle Ranch." Ed pointed in my direction.

"What?" I turned to Oscar. "What's he talking about?" I thought I must have made an involuntary motion, and I stood to explain.

"I don't think you did anything," Oscar said, reading my mind.

"What's going on?" I prepared to approach someone. But Ed finished his announcement.

"Congratulations, Mr. Bob Arbuckle."

I froze for a moment, then turned, and ten rows behind us, there sat Bob, with Helen right next to him, looking as innocent as could be. She smiled and Bob lowered his eyes, and an anger rose up inside me like I hadn't felt in a long time.

"I need to take a walk. I need to get out of here," I said to Oscar.

"Okay."

We left the building and I couldn't think straight. I paced back and forth. I paced. I paced.

"Don't you handle the stock?" Oscar asked.

I nodded, too angry to speak.

Oscar looked at his boots. The sun reflected off his glasses. "Shouldn't you talk to Bob?"

I looked up, frowning.

Oscar cleared his throat. "If I was you, I'd want to ask what the hell he's thinking. He must have some idea in his head."

"Yeah, well…I guess everyone has their own way of dealing with these things."

"Fair enough." Oscar nodded, pushing his glasses up his nose. "So what are you gonna do?"

I was surprised how much this question bothered me, especially when I realized that I had no idea how to answer. I didn't know what to do. In fact, it hadn't even occurred to me to do something. My thought leaned more toward enduring.

"What would you do?" I asked.

Oscar brightened. "Well…like I said…I'd ask Bob what he's thinking. Maybe he's got something in mind. Like turning around and selling them. Maybe he knows someone who's crazy enough to spend even more. Why else would he do that? He's got just as much at stake in the ranch as you do, right?"

I was tempted to explain to Oscar why Bob would do this. Or more accurately, why Helen would do it. But his questions got me wondering whether I could be wrong. Besides, I still didn't feel like I knew Oscar well enough to tell him the whole story yet.

"Let's go." I headed back toward the building.

"Okay…you're the boss."

As we climbed the steps toward Bob and Helen, I watched the color drain from Bob's face. He looked around, searching for a way to escape. But Helen met my eye with the self-satisfied expression I'd come to despise in the years since she'd joined our family. Her look said, 'If you even think about accusing me of something, I'll shoot you down before you know what hit you. I'm three steps ahead of you, and you know it.'

And I did know. A part of me had no desire to fight her, because fighting meant learning to think the same way she thought. I had no interest in learning her game.

I made a beeline for the seat next to my brother. Oscar sat on the other side of me. Bob's leg started bouncing like it used to do when a younger Bob couldn't wait to visit Helen after supper.

"Aren't those some of the most beautiful cattle you've ever seen?" Helen leaned around Bob.

Oscar laughed. "That's the first time I've heard cows called beautiful."

"But they are," Helen said. "They really are beautiful."

"Not sure they're eighty dollars' worth of beautiful," I said.

"Sure they are," Helen said. "Besides, it was only seventy-seven."

I watched the bidding on forty head that were almost as nice as our new herd. Fifty dollars.

"You've dug a pretty big hole there, Bob."

"Those are by far the best cattle here," Helen said. "I don't see how buying the best cattle here could be digging a hole."

I turned to my brother. "Is that how you see it, Bob?"

Bob's jaw worked, chewing the inside of his cheek to ground beef. But he didn't answer or meet my eye.

"Fitty-five, fitty-five, fitty-five, do I hear fitty-seven..."

"So what do you got in mind for these cattle, Bob?" I asked.

Bob fidgeted. "I don't know. Feed 'em. Breed 'em. I'm not sure what you mean, Blake."

"What an odd question," Helen said.

Oscar watched this exchange with a baffled expression.

"Well, if we're gonna be paying this kind of money for these cattle, I'd like to know what you got in mind for them," I said.

"Oh, you're not paying for these cattle," Helen said. "These are our cattle. We're buying these."

Chapter 5

The Days of '85 in Ekalaka is one of the highlights of our year in Carter County. As one of the few chances we get to see almost everyone we know, this event provides an opportunity for people to parade their new clothes, catch up on the latest gossip, or lose a little of our hard-earned cash at the carnival, or the horse races. All in two days.

This year, with so much abundance, we heard juicy stories about people buying cars that were too expensive, clothes that were too flashy, and boots made of exotic animal skins–rhinoceros and crocodile. We heard about one rancher near Deadwood whose big new house featured gold-plated fixtures. Many disapproved. I couldn't help but wonder, after so many years of struggling, whether some people were getting carried away with celebrating their success. As if they were going to suck as much out of life as they could while the good times lasted.

But the biggest story of this particular day swirled around a mysterious fellow who had entered a horse in the afternoon's race. Captain Andy had won several races around the region, all in convincing fashion. Most of us hadn't had a chance to see him run yet.

Dad didn't feel up to coming along, but he didn't like Rita's offer to stay home with him one bit. So he was back at the house, grouchy and alone.

"What the hell is this?" Teddy pointed his fork at a pile of food on his plate.

"It's a casserole," Margie said.

"Does it have any actual food in it, you think?" Teddy asked.

Margie giggled. Steve was also absent this year, and none of us had to ask why. Teddy had confided that getting

Margie to come had been a struggle. She didn't want to face the sympathetic stares.

"Why did you take it if you didn't like how it looked?" she asked Teddy.

"It was the mystery of it," Teddy said.

Margie laughed, and I was glad to see them so relaxed.

"Did you enter the rodeo, Oscar?" I asked.

"Maybe," he said.

"Oh, really? I was actually kidding."

Oscar winked. "Maybe I am, too."

We gorged on every form of beast, vegetable, and sugar known to man until we lay immobilized with food. Then we napped as the sun settled in the center of the clear blue sky. When I wasn't dozing, I watched our neighbors sauntering around the grounds.

Tex Winters walked by with his fourth wife Angie, who was twenty years younger and wore a blue dress with a bow as big as an airplane.

"Did you hear that Tex was trying to buy the Christoph place?" Rita asked.

I nodded. "No big surprise."

Rita shook her head. "Some people are never satisfied."

"Let's just hope this wife survives a few years," Teddy mumbled.

"Ooh, that was mean," Margie said with delight. There had been rumors for years about Tex's second wife, who came from a wealthy family and drowned in a puddle about four inches deep. The local sheriff, not known for being effective, couldn't prove a thing.

People milled toward the grandstands, and the announcer climbed into his booth and introduced the bareback bronc riding. I kept an eye on Oscar the whole afternoon, wondering whether he would sneak off and appear in the middle of the arena. But when he didn't show up during calf roping, I had a feeling I knew which event he'd entered.

The rodeo featured several fine moments. One of the bareback bronc riders drew Thundercloud, a legendary horse that had a unique bucking style, hopping straight up into the air. This rider stayed with the bronc with each lunge, his left hand anchoring him to the sorrel's broad back. But halfway through the eight seconds, the horse made a sudden shift, twisting to one side. The cowboy flew into the air, and except for his left hand, he dangled so far off the horse that it seemed impossible for him to avoid being thrown. But in a show of amazing strength, he managed to pull himself toward the horse, at the same time rotating his body so he came down on the horse's rump. On the next buck, he lurched forward to the middle of Thundercloud's back. The horn blew and we rose to our feet, cheering and whistling, shouting his name. But the cowboy picked up his hat and walked out of the arena as if he'd just finished milking a cow.

The other highlight came when a local steer wrestler who had finished in the money at several rodeos broke the string, leaned off his horse, and landed on the steer's neck almost before the string hit the ground. He slid off his saddle, and his heels dug into the arena dirt as he wrapped both arms around the steer's horns. With a single twist of his body, the steer flipped onto his back. His time--three seconds. The grandstands shook.

Rita had been sitting very close to me all afternoon. She occasionally locked her hand into the crook of my elbow and even rested her head against my shoulder. These public displays of affection were unusual, and a bit embarrassing. I assumed she was happy to be sharing our first Days of '85 as a couple. But about the time that the bull riding started, she leaned over and whispered in my ear.

"You know how much I love you, Blake Arbuckle?"

My face got hot, but I managed to say, "Of course, sweetheart."

"I have something to tell you," she breathed.

"Oh?"

She nestled up against me. "I'm going to have a baby."

I couldn't even begin to respond. A rider fell hard just before the horn sounded. I watched him limp toward the chutes, hand on a bruised hip. I couldn't look at Rita. I couldn't speak. Rita was forty-five years old. I was forty-six. I had dismissed the possibility of having a child years ago. When I finally spoke, I muttered, "What did you say?"

Rita chuckled. "You heard me."

"Are you sure?"

She laughed again. "Mr. Arbuckle, I suggest you take my word on this."

"Wow…that's terrific. That's really terrific, honey. It's terrific."

"Isn't it?" Rita smiled, her green eyes squinting up at me, and I just had to give her a big kiss on the cheek, right there in front of ninety percent of Carter County. And for the rest of the day, I felt a warmth in my gut that I couldn't have possibly expressed in words. I had given up on the idea of being a father years ago, and here we were. It didn't seem possible.

The announcer bawled out the last event of the day. "Ladies and gentlemen, it's time for the wild horse race!"

Seven teams perched at the ready, and of course Oscar was among them, teamed up with two Belle Fourche cowboys. The bell sounded, and Oscar pounced from the fence, wrapping himself around their horse's neck like wet paper. The horse threw its head, but Oscar hung on, and reached for the horse's right ear, leaning up, taking it in his mouth and biting down like a cornered dog. While the other horses thrashed in their chutes, this one froze, and one of Oscar's teammates dropped a saddle onto the horse's back. The other reached in between the planks and grabbed the cinch, pulling it under the horse's belly with a long piece of bent wire. The horse suddenly threw his head, but Oscar didn't budge. His muscular little body tensed, his arms locked tighter, and his neck showed the strain as he bit down harder. The horse went still again, and the other cowboy tightened the cinch.

Oscar then reached for the bridle, let go of the ear, then slipped the bridle over the horse's head before it had a chance to protest. Oscar hopped onto the fence while one of his partners lowered himself into the saddle. The third swung the gate open.

Their team was so far ahead of the others that the rider had the whole arena to himself for a good twenty seconds. The horse bucked and raced around, trying to rid himself of this burden. As it turned out, only two other riders managed to stay on their horses. But Oscar's team won easily, and moments later Oscar climbed into the stands holding up three silver dollars, shouting, "When do the real races start?"

"You're crazy," I said.

Oscar's laugh echoed across the grandstand. "Yes I am."

After soaking up some glory, Oscar bounded down the stairs to find the betting window for the horse racing. I leaned over to my wife, still cuddled up to me. "I heard the strangest rumor about an hour ago."

"Oh?"

"Yeah, it was just ridiculous."

She giggled, an outburst more girlish than I'd ever heard from her. And it charmed the hell out of me.

A half hour after the rodeo ended, the arena filled up and a tractor circled the track several times, dragging a rake to smooth it over. A row of horses filed out from the barn behind the grandstands. Each horse, led by its trainer, sported a dusty cowboy perched on a tiny racing saddle. In the twenties, the locals had built a racing gate, and the races had become quite an attraction. Since the war ended, several local ranchers had invested in top quality quarter horses, making the races more competitive, and bringing out big wagers. We'd heard at least one story about a rancher losing his place because he'd bet too much on the ponies. Not everyone was happy with these developments, but when the time for the races came around, they seemed to forget about that.

The crowd murmured, wondering which horse was Captain Andy, until it became quite evident. Even among this better-than-average gathering of horses, one strode with a majesty we seldom saw. His black coat looked wet. The muscles in his haunches appeared etched into his coat. He even carried himself differently, as if insulted about performing on such a small stage, to such an insignificant crowd. Between the murmurings you could almost feel our shame about subjecting him to this. I studied my program.

Captain Andy had lost only one of the seven races he'd entered. He finished third in that one, but someone near us said that the track was 'muddier than an escaped convict on a riverbank.'

Eight horses had entered the race. Captain Andy danced in the fourth position and when the bell rattled, he broke late, strolling out of the gate a good second behind the other horses. As the other seven strained through the first twenty yards, Captain Andy's first strides stretched out in an even, steady rhythm. His head bobbed, as if he was rocking it to a song that only he could hear. A horse called Texas Wind pulled five yards in front of the pack, then angled over to the rail. The other six horses bunched up behind Texas Wind, and Captain Andy loped behind them, running so easily that he appeared to be surveying the scenery. His jockey did not push him at all. Texas Wind pulled another five yards in front, and a stringy gray horse drifted back.

Then Captain Andy's jockey nudged him, and he kicked into another gear. With an almost imperceptible change in tempo, his muscles rippled as he moved like a wave, surging, receding, surging, receding, his head bobbing faster with each stride. He passed the gray straggler, and after they rounded the far turn, he broke to the outside and rushed past the pack of five with a handful of massive lunges.

Texas Wind must have heard the pounding hooves behind him. He sped up, his jockey thumping his rump, but this horse did not possess the same fluid ease. You could almost see Texas Wind's teeth clench. While Captain Andy's nose moved forward with each stride, as if it were leading the way, pulling him forward, Texas Wind's neck strained down toward his knees, as if he might trip over his own jaw.

Texas Wind pulled away from the rest of the field, but Captain Andy galloped by him as if Texas Wind had found a patch of gumbo. Coming down the stretch, the dirt barely stirred under Captain Andy's hooves. He crossed the line eight lengths in front.

We screamed. And most of the faces in the crowd smiled, either because they bet on the right horse or because we had just witnessed such an amazing spectacle. Oscar held his ticket high above his head, not caring that the odds were so low that his payoff would only be a few thin dimes.

People gathered around Captain Andy, shaking hands and running their palms along Captain Andy's sleek coat. I felt a strong sense of familiarity with one of the men in the middle of the gathering.

"Oh my god."

Rita looked over at me. "What?"

"Look." I nodded toward the gathering.

Rita shaded her eyes and gazed at the scene, squinting. "What, Blake? I don't see what you mean." She looked at me again.

"Jack," I said.

Her head jerked toward the track and a moment later she muttered, "Jesus."

"It looks like he's part of the crew," I said. "Like he's with the horse."

She nodded. "It does, doesn't it?"

I checked my program, running my finger down the names of owners, and trainers, and when I came to Captain Andy, I read that the owner lived in Miles City. But when I moved over to the column where the other names were listed, my heart stopped. I nudged Rita.

"What?"

I pointed at the program.

"David Westford? Oh my god."

David Westford was a man I had met on a train ride to Omaha when I was sixteen. He would be best described as a man of unbridled appetites. He was huge, and rich, and offered to buy me the services of a prostitute. Two of them, actually. By some remarkable coincidence, the same David Westford had met my brother Jack years later and became his partner in a scheme to extort supplies from the US Army and sell them on the black market. But at this moment, what mattered was the name Jack used when he re-enlisted in the Army as part of their plan—David Westford.

I thought back to the last I'd heard anything about Jack, when an investigator from the Army had come to our house looking for him. I had assumed in the two years since he'd disappeared that he was probably in prison. Now he looked almost unrecognizable, fuller but older.

"What are you guys looking at?" Teddy leaned toward me.

"Nothing," I said.

"Nothing?" He laughed. "Come on. What is it?"

"It really is nothing," Rita said.

Teddy studied the crowd but he wasn't interested enough to try very hard, and I was thankful he didn't recognize his father.

"Well, I'm hungry," Teddy said. "Margie, you ready to eat?"

"Didn't we just do that?" Margie moaned.

Teddy took her hand. "Honey, that was at least thirty minutes ago. Come on."

Rita and I stood and silently watched my older brother as they took pictures, then turned Captain Andy around and started to lead him toward the barn. Jack walked on the other side of Captain Andy and he looked up into the crowd for a moment. It may have been my imagination, but I think our eyes met. All I know is that in the next instant, he looked away.

After supper, a band started sawing away with a fiddle, a bass, a slide guitar, and a piano. They featured two excellent singers and welcomed volunteers to come up and warble. I dragged Rita to the floor and wouldn't let her leave. Not that she put up a fight. We wrapped our arms around each other and whirled around the floor until bands of sweat crossed our backs. I kept an eye out for Jack but didn't see any sign of him.

"You having fun?" Rita asked after a few songs.

"Not really."

She smiled. "I can tell."

"You?"

"Me neither."

"Yeah, this has been a horrible day."

"We should've stayed home."

"Let's try and remember that next year, all right?"

We shook hands.

I noticed that Oscar didn't dance, preferring to sit at a table in the corner where he talked intently with anyone who joined him. But Teddy, Margie, Bob and Helen hit the floor just as much as we did. I soaked in the atmosphere, hoping against all reason that the good will that filled that dance hall would carry over into the next day, the next week, the next year. It's a weakness of mine, this idea that families will always get along, that people will appreciate what's good about each other and ignore the rest.

When we finally took a break I sat next to Oscar, who was visiting with a neighbor.

"What's the story, fellas?" I asked.

"I was just telling Oscar here that I lost money on you," the neighbor said.

"Oh?"

"Thought it was a safe bet, too."

"Let me guess," I said.

"Yeah, most of us thought that Blake here would be the only guy we knew who never jumped the broomstick."

"I would have made that bet myself if I'd known about it," I said.

"So how did you meet Rita?" Oscar asked.

"Oh, she just sort of showed up," I said.

My neighbor chuckled.

"I'll tell you the whole story sometime," I said. "When we have a couple of days."

"You have a lot of stories like that," Oscar said.

The discussion brought Jack back into my thoughts, and I made another quick scan of the dance floor. As much as Jack loved to dance, I was surprised he wasn't there. But I certainly didn't want to see him. Not with everything coming together for our little family.

I decided to escape back to the dance floor, and I tracked Rita down outside. The sky was spotless, or I should say cloudless, covered with tiny, bright stars. I could smell hay as if my face were buried in a meadow, and even with the music echoing from inside, I could still hear the crickets.

"How you doin'?" I asked Rita.

"It's so nice out here." She tilted her head against my shoulder.

"You ready to dance a little?" I asked.

"You know someone who's interested?"

"No, but I can ask around, see if someone's sitting off by themselves."

"Aren't you the gentleman?"

"I have my moments."

I took Rita's hand, leading her inside. Just as we entered, a sudden commotion erupted from one corner of the hall. People moved in a wave, murmuring, and Jack came to mind again. But I was shocked when I saw the foes standing toe to toe, red-faced and glaring—Bob and Oscar.

I pushed to the front of the crowd. "What the hell's going on here?"

"You better ask him." Oscar tipped his head toward Bob.

I turned to Bob, who looked embarrassed. He didn't answer the question, or meet my eye. He simply turned and left. I looked around for Helen but saw no sign of her. So I led Oscar outside.

"What happened?"

"Good question," he said. "He was standing in my face, asking me to step outside, before I even recognized who it was."

I frowned, thinking that this didn't sound like anything that Bob had ever done. "He didn't say anything else?"

"Well, I asked him what the problem was and all he said was, 'You think you can just walk onto our place and become the big hero? Push the rest of us to the side?'"

"Hmm." I buried my fists in my pockets.

I asked someone nearby if they'd heard anything. They verified Oscar's version.

When Rita and I made our way back to the dance floor, I told her what Oscar said.

"Oh, that doesn't surprise me."

"It doesn't?"

"Blake, haven't you noticed how Bob and Helen act around him?"

"No. What are you talking about?"

"They can't stand him, Blake."

"How can they not like Oscar? He's perfectly harmless."

Rita leaned away from me just enough to look up at my face. This amused expression had become a familiar one since we got married. "I love you, Blake Arbuckle, but you can be pretty thick sometimes."

"What do you mean?"

"You really don't know what's going on, do you?"

"Tell me."

Rita craned her neck, checking for Bob and Helen. She tilted her head toward them. "They want the ranch, Blake. They, or I should say 'she'...won't be happy with anything less."

"No," I said.

Rita kissed my cheek. "I love it that you don't understand. And I love it that no amount of explaining will make any difference."

I blushed, embarrassed and confused by her flattery. I felt stupid. "But what does all that have to do with Oscar?"

She grabbed my cheeks. "He's part of us, Blake. We're the enemy, and he's part of us."

I sighed, then shook my head. "I don't believe that."

Rita just nodded. "I know you don't."

We two-stepped to the strains of "Walkin' the Floor Over You," our bodies rocking with the beat. The crowd had thinned, but not much. Most of them would dance until dawn. The smell of alcohol became stronger by the hour.

The laughter got louder, the skin more flushed. There was not a face in the building that didn't have a thin sheen of sweat.

"What do you think we should do?" I asked Rita.

"We have to fight back."

"Yeah, I guess." I shook my head. "As if blizzards and hailstorms don't give us enough drama around here."

Chapter 6

For several weeks, Rita and I kept our pending arrival to ourselves. But one evening as fall began to suck the color from the grass, we sat down with Teddy and told him the news. He looked at us as if it hadn't even occurred to him that we were actually married. I could only imagine his thoughts, as a young man old enough to become a father himself. He didn't respond for quite a while, looking at his mother with his mouth half-open.

"Wow," he finally said. "When?"

"March," Rita said.

"So he'll be ready to help with the harvest."

I watched Rita break into a smile, releasing an inner anxiety about how her son would react. "How do you know it's a boy?"

"Because we need the help around here, and I know how considerate you are, Mom."

Rita punched him in the arm.

That same evening, we roused Dad from his early evening doze. "Pop, what do you think about becoming a grandfather again?" I asked.

"Did Bob and Helen finally get it right?" he asked, blinking.

"No...it's us, Dad," Rita answered.

He frowned. "You two?" He shook his head.

"You don't want another grandkid?" I asked.

"Just another fist pulling at my wallet," he muttered, but one corner of his mouth curled.

"Dad, you're awful," Rita said.

"Well hopefully, it will be a girl so you can get some help around here," he said, and Rita's cheek flushed.

A few days later, just after supper, Rita and I took the short walk across the rock-hard gumbo driveway to Bob and Helen's house. When Helen answered the door, it was the first time I've ever seen her speechless. We had not been to their home for about two years. And vice versa. Soon after we discovered that Bob and Helen had stolen money from the ranch to buy furniture, the effort to even pretend that we got along had left the barn. In a country where people rely so much on family, it felt wrong, and odd. But the thirty yards between our two homes had become a journey none of us wanted to make. When your only neighbors are also your relatives, it can be a blessing in the best of times. But when things are going badly, the proximity only magnifies the cancer. So our two houses stood like lovers in a quarrel, backs to each other, arms folded.

Helen gathered her composure. "Come in."

We exchanged stiff formalities before Helen summoned Bob from wherever he was hiding. Bob scratched the back of his head and sank into a chair across the room from Helen. She perched on the sofa.

"Well, there's no use pretending this is a social call," Rita said. "We came over to tell you some news—something we wanted you to hear from us." She swallowed. "I'm going to have a baby."

Helen's back straightened slowly, like an animal whose life has been threatened. "Isn't that nice?"

Bob shifted in his chair, leaning as far away from Helen as he could, although he was on the other side of the room. Helen's round cheeks went red, shining as if they'd been polished. A short silence followed.

I spoke up. "Well. I guess we oughta be going. We just wanted to let you know."

"Well, we certainly do appreciate that," Helen said. "But aren't you a little concerned…with your age and all?"

Bob covered his face, rubbing it as if he held a washcloth.

"Excuse me?" Rita tilted her head to one side.

"Well, of course it's none of my business, but if I was you, I just think it would be a concern."

Rita sat up.

"We've talked to the doctor about that," I lied. "So we know the risks."

"That's right," Rita said.

"Well, good," Helen said. "You can never be too careful." Although this seemed like the closest thing to an honest to God show of sincere concern that I'd ever seen from Helen, I didn't want to push it.

"We really should be going," I said. "We'll see you at Glasser's."

Bob nodded, looking guilty about any response at all.

Rita and I started for the door.

"It's not going to work, you know," Helen said.

Rita spun. "Work?"

Helen smiled, her tiny mouth bending into a tight curl. "It's not going to work."

"We'll see you," I said, grabbing Rita's arm.

After fighting my wife's desire to go back inside, I slammed the door behind us. And we stood on the stoop staring at each other.

"Well, I guess if it wasn't obvious already…we are in some kind of war," Rita said.

"Apparently so."

"When did that happen?"

"I think it probably started the minute she walked down the aisle."

The next Monday was hot for September, with the temperature hovering around seventy degrees. The Glassers had invested in a new thresher and the improvement was dramatic. It could handle half again as much grain as the old model. Even so, with the fields yielding a higher percentage, harvest would take two or three long days.

I spent the first morning holding burlap between my knees, gripping the edges tightly while the grain flowed into the open mouth. The skin on my fingers had cracked, leaving blood on the burlap. I looked forward to rotating jobs after dinner.

We moved at a faster pace than usual, the grain flowing in a thick golden stream from the chute. The unseasonable heat seemed to dry up any potential conversation.

"More to the left," Oscar shouted. "No! The left!"

Holding the swelling burlap between my legs, I saw him sitting on top of the thresher, gesturing wildly with one hand. "Hurry…Jesus!" He jumped down and rushed around the machine, out of my view. I closed the gate on the chute and raced around the thresher, just in time to see Oscar drive a shoulder into Bob, tackling him.

"Whoa!" I shouted. "What the hell is going on?"

I grabbed Oscar by the shoulder, trying to pull him to the side. It was like trying to move a damn house. I leaned, to put more of my body into the effort, when Bob's fist suddenly shot up and caught Oscar right in the nose.

"Hey!" In a quick, powerful motion, Oscar caught both of Bob's wrists and pinned him to the ground, leaning over him with the force of his muscular weight. "I was trying to help, you goddam fool. That belt's going to come loose, and it was about to take your head off."

A few drops of blood dripped from Oscar's nose onto Bob's forehead. Oscar turned his head to one side and wiped his nose on his shoulder. I stepped away from them. Steve shut down the thresher and the crew gathered.

"Why don't you let him up?" I said.

"You okay?" Oscar asked Bob.

Bob nodded. Oscar freed Bob's hands, and leaned back.

"You calm, Bob?" I asked.

"Yeah, I'm all right." Bob looked at Oscar from the side of his eyes.

"It's probably a good time to break for dinner," Steve said.

Margie, Helen, and Rita had laid out plates of ham sandwiches, fried potatoes, pickles and applesauce. We'd heard that Jenny would not be home anytime soon.

We ate with focus, our bodies hungry after a hard morning. The table would have been as quiet as the meadow if not for the hum of the Glasser's generator. And Oscar.

"I haven't seen wheat this nice in my whole life," he said. "Those heads are like pumpkins."

Everyone nodded.

"It is the best year we've ever had," Steve agreed.

"And prices are up," Oscar added.

"It's a hard time for us pessimists," I said.

"I remember my dad talking about the watershed years back in the old country," Oscar said. "I always wondered whether I'd ever get a chance to see what he meant."

"We damn sure earned it," I said.

"I'll tell you what, though..." Oscar wiped his mouth. "Nothing makes you appreciate good times like living through the bad...you lose your damn wife, it puts you in a daze for a while, but when you come out of it and realize you got a whole lotta world sitting out there waiting for you, it makes you think."

Bob muttered under his breath. Then there was silence as we focused on our food. By the time we were ready to head back to the fields, the silence had still not broken.

"I'm not sure we're gonna get done today," Steve said as we started out the door.

"Ah, come on, Steve. Plenty of daylight left. Lots of time." Oscar clasped his hands together.

"Listen, buster..." Bob stopped, pointing at Oscar. "Maybe you're grateful for all the damn suffering in the world, but some of us are a little tired of it...some of us just want to get through the day, all right?"

Oscar stopped, holding out his hands. "What are you talking about?"

"Why don't you just shut your yap for once," Bob mumbled.

"Did you lose your damn baby bottle or something? What did I ever do to you?" Oscar asked.

Helen stepped forward. "Mr. MacArthur, I would ask you to show some respect for my husband."

"Mrs. Arbuckle, for one thing, I saved your husband's life this morning. And for another, where I come from, respect is something you gotta earn. I just say what's on my mind, which isn't a crime in Montana, as far as I know."

"No...you're right, Mr. MacArthur...it's not a crime. But that doesn't mean everyone should do it."

"You're entitled to your opinion, Mrs. Arbuckle. That doesn't mean I have to follow it."

"Don't talk to my wife that way," Bob muttered.

Oscar frowned. "I really have no idea what your problem is, Bob."

I watched Bob's jaw tighten, hands flexing, curling into the beginnings of fists. I stepped between the two men. "Easy, Bob."

"Why don't you mind your own business for once, Blake?" Bob met my gaze but his eyes jumped back and forth.

"This is my business, Bob. You're both part of this ranch, and that makes it my business."

Helen looked up at me. "Blake, maybe you haven't been paying attention, but this is not your ranch, and furthermore, your brother is not a child anymore."

"I'm not talking to him like a child, and I don't think Oscar is either. I really don't understand what triggered all of this."

Suddenly, a voice exploded from behind. "How much longer are you all gonna cut into our workday with this bickering?" Steve glared at us all, red-faced, his eyes wide. The skewed one veered off like it didn't want any part of any of us. "Are we gonna harvest, or are we gonna stand around arguing about who's the biggest child?"

We shuffled toward the back door, our faces reflecting varying degrees of irritation and shame, and by the time Helen got in the last word it was fairly lost in the heavy air. "That's not at all what we were talking about, Steve."

The silence that had been only slightly tense all morning had twisted up like a rope by the time we got back to the fields. But instead of bringing our focus closer to our work, it made us all distracted, watching Bob and Oscar warily.

I sat at my new post, next to the engine, where I had to keep an eye on the belt. Just above me, an old pitchfork handle held a wet burlap bag to attract mosquitoes. I reached up and shook it now and then. Although my task required constant scrutiny, and occasionally shutting down the machine to realign the belt, it was mostly a monotonous job, and as the afternoon passed, the sound of the engine felt as if it had vibrated into my head. Bob was bagging and Oscar loaded the bags. They did not talk. When a bag filled, Bob tied the top. Oscar crouched in front of him and hefted the bag to his shoulder, then carried it to the truck.

Harvest has always been my favorite time of year, with the satisfaction of holding onto such tangible results of our labor. I love watching the grain rush like water from the thresher, and the weight of a full burlap bag on my back. But it is also exhausting, and by the end of that day, I watched with relief as the sun sank slowly toward the horizon. When we loaded up and drove back to Glassers, my body was clenched like a fist. I thought I might fall asleep in my food.

"Are you okay?" Rita asked.

"I don't know. What a strange day."

"You know we need to keep an eye on that woman, don't you?" She gestured vaguely toward Bob and Helen's house with her fork.

"No more than usual."

But Rita shook her head. "No, Blake. It's worse. She's got something cooking."

"Not like you." I put a hand to her belly. "How are you feeling?"

She smiled. "You're trying to change the subject, aren't you, Blake Arbuckle."

"Maybe."

"Well, before you do that, something happened today. I went out to get the mail, and there was a letter addressed to Bob and Helen. From Jack."

This brought my fork up short of my mouth. "Really?"

Rita nodded.

"You're sure?"

She lowered her chin, looking at me from the top of her eyes.

"Okay, I guess you would know your ex-husband's handwriting."

"Thank you."

"Wow. I wonder what that's about."

"Well, I think it's a safe bet that it's not good."

Chapter 7

On the Wednesday before Thanksgiving, riding in from the fields, I spotted Stan and Muriel's car in front of the house, and a smile came to my face. "Ha!" I shouted.

Oscar jumped, then followed my gaze. "Who is it?"

"My sister Muriel and her family."

"Oh really? I didn't know they were coming." Oscar smiled, giving Patsy a little nudge with his heels.

I entered the house with a hearty "Hello!" before I could even see who might be within shouting distance. Stan's signature "Ha!" echoed through the house, and again, the smile stretched across my face. Rita, Muriel, Teddy, Dad, and Stan had gathered around the dining room table. Dad and Teddy were playing cribbage.

Stan rose, rounding the table with his hand extended. "Great to see you, Blake."

"Likewise." We shook like we meant it, and I hugged my sister.

"How you guys doing?" I asked.

"Life is good," Stan said. "Rita's been filling us in on things. Sounds like things are going well here, too." He pointed at Rita's stomach.

I tilted my head from side to side. "Can't complain."

"I'd have to slap you if you did," Stan said.

"Stan!" Muriel whacked his arm.

"Where's the kids?" I asked.

"Oh, they're out exploring." Stan gestured vaguely outside. "Probably tracking a bear or something."

"I'm surprised we didn't see them on our way in."

"Hell, they could be anywhere," Stan said.

"I think I saw 'em headed for the shop," Oscar said, easing up behind me.

"By the way, this is Oscar. I've probably mentioned him."

"Superhand, right?" Stan offered Oscar his hand.

Oscar blushed, and I swear his glasses steamed up. "I don't know about that." He quickly excused himself, explaining that he needed to get cleaned up. His face burned red.

"That guy feels like he's carved out of wood," Stan said.

"Stan!" Muriel said again.

"He's solid," I said, laughing. "You run into any weather?"

"Some snow near Bozeman," Muriel said.

"It got pretty cloudy the last fifty miles," Stan added.

As we spent the next hour getting caught up, a wind began whistling around the house. Muriel checked the clock a few times, and when a gust shook the walls, she took Stan's elbow.

"I'll go check on them," I said.

"Oh would you, Blake?"

"I'll go with you," Stan offered.

"That's okay."

"No, Blake," Muriel insisted. "Take Stan along."

"Well, he better promise not to whine about the cold."

Stan winked at Muriel. "I promise."

I threw on my winter coat and grabbed my scotch cap. Stan wrapped himself in a knee-length camel hair coat.

"Planning on doing some campaigning while you're here?" I asked.

Stan smiled, draping a scarf around his neck. He tugged a fedora down over his eyes. "What would I run for? Mayor of Albion?"

We laughed at the thought of Albion, a town that consisted of three buildings, needing any government.

When we stepped out into the fading light, the temperature had dropped at least twenty degrees since my ride home. An east wind stung our cheeks.

"Damn, we might not have enough clothes," I said.

"I think you're right."

We headed for the barn and the wind picked up, pushing against us, sucking air from our lungs. We shouted the kids' names, and the sound just died.

"We might have quite a storm coming," Stan said.

"Feels like it."

By the time we got to the barn, we felt snow in the air. Specks of white flew past. Inside the barn, we yelled for the kids. Our echo was the only response.

"Maybe we ought to split up," Stan suggested. "I'll check the grain elevator, and…what do you think? The shop?"

"Okay."

Outside we walked together until the fork in the driveway, continuing to throw the kids' names out into the cold wind. Then we split.

"Meet me here either way," I said.

"You got it."

With our little cluster of buildings sitting in the middle of nowhere, the wind attacked our homestead with a relentless force—pushing, pushing, pushing. I entered the shop, relieved to be free of the icy air rubbing against my face. The air vibrated, as if the walls could collapse at any moment. I called out and again got no response. When I stepped back outside, wet specks snapped against my cheek, and it felt like sand. The flakes were thick, flying through the silky black sky at angles.

When Stan didn't appear at the fork in the driveway, I started toward the grain elevator, calling out for Stan along with the kids. But the elevator was empty.

I ran out to the driveway, pacing back and forth, shouting as loud as the cold air would allow. The snow multiplied, and the air felt like cold metal. My lungs hurt when I yelled. When I saw no sign of them, I ran to the house, bursting inside.

"Have you seen them?" I asked before I even saw anyone.

Dorothy, their youngest, appeared in the dining room doorway. "Hi, Uncle Blake!"

"Where's your brothers?"

"Over there." She pointed toward the living room.

"Oh, thank God."

Muriel rounded the corner into the kitchen, relief showing on her face. But her expression quickly shifted. "Where's Stan?"

"He's not here?"

"No."

"Didn't he bring the kids in?"

"No, they came in a few minutes after you left."

"Damn." I turned. "I'll be right back."

"Blake, you should take someone with you," Muriel called.

"I'll go." I heard Oscar's voice, but I couldn't wait.

Outside, the wind had become nothing but snow. It flew so thick that I had to fold my arm around my face, peering over my elbow. I had to trust my instincts for direction. I held a hand straight out in front of me, at eye level, for protection, and kept my gaze to the ground, looking for landmarks. I bumped into something at my waist, and found the hitching post. I worked my way around that and stumbled in the direction of the grain elevator.

A voice cried out in my head to think about what I was doing. I knew Stan hadn't been in the elevator moments before. Going to the elevator made no sense. I couldn't guess where he'd gone from there. These facts alone made looking for him ridiculous. I knew I should go back.

But I pushed forward, leaning into the wind, calling Stan's name. I heard a voice from behind, shouting my name. I turned, looking for Stan. The relief from the wind allowed me to breathe. But instead of Stan, I saw the hunched, muscular figure of Oscar MacArthur striding through the wind. He caught up and took my elbow in his formidable grasp. He leaned close.

"You need to go back, Blake. This is crazy."

He held something, and I leaned down to see a rope, which he had tied to something back at the house.

I shook my head. "We've got to find him, Oscar."

Despite yelling as loud as we could, we barely heard each other.

"Do you know where he was going?"

I shook my head.

"Blake, come on. We can't go out there if you don't know where he is."

"Ten minutes, Oscar. Let's give it ten minutes."

Oscar squinted, reaching up in a vain attempt to rub the snow from his glasses. Instead, he smeared the moisture around until the lenses were almost white.

"All right, Blake. Ten minutes." He gripped my elbow tighter, until it hurt. "Don't lose me, Blake."

I nodded, then turned and leaned toward the grain elevator, moving my legs so that they caught up with my torso. Oscar's fingers dug into my muscle but I ignored the pain, trying to see, pushing hard against the wind. Oscar moved past me, his knees rising high to compensate for his short legs. He pulled me along. We staggered forward, tripping over drifts, and unidentified objects. Something dark emerged. Oscar reached out to find a wall. We got close enough to see that we'd found the shop. We had drifted ninety degrees too far to the west.

I tipped my head toward the building, indicating we should go inside, and Oscar nodded.

We felt our way along the rough surface, not even sure which direction we should go. In my eagerness to reach our destination, I ran into Oscar. Finally, Oscar's gloved hand touched the door frame. He leaned into the door, and fell forward when it gave much easier than he expected. I slipped in and helped Oscar to his feet, and he had to put all of his weight into the door to get it closed.

We both sat, breathing cold, icy air, our arms like corpses on our laps. I twisted my neck around, looking for Stan. The building shook as if it could fly into the air at any moment, but the shop was deathly quiet compared to the storm outside.

"We need to get back to the house," Oscar said.

"We can't leave him out here." I lay back, stunned by fatigue and helplessness. I hated this feeling more than anything. As much as I wanted to argue, I knew Oscar was right. We rested for a few minutes, then rolled to our hands and knees and slowly rose to our feet.

"I hate to do it, Oscar. I really hate to do it."

"I know, Blake."

With the wind to our backs, the return trip was like walking downhill. I kept turning around, looking behind me. Each time, the wind smacked me in the face, watering my eyes so that I couldn't have seen even if the snow wasn't blurring my vision.

We poured into the house to anxious faces. And our expressions answered their question.

"Oh God." Muriel sank into a chair.

"Where's Daddy?" Dorothy asked.

"He's still outside," I said. "He'll be back soon." I delivered this hopeful lie with almost no enthusiasm, although it seemed to satisfy Dorothy.

The wind howled for the rest of the evening. Every time I looked out the window, the snow covered the scene like a white sheet. It piled toward the windowsills. No one spoke, which made the whir and groan of the generator and the crackle of the fire even louder. The stony tension eventually dampened the children's enthusiasm. They stopped playing and sat in a row on the couch, watching us with worried expressions until Muriel whisked them off to bed. They didn't protest.

I had to battle my desire to go back outside. Rita approached me a couple times, trying to give me a little hug, or say something comforting. But I couldn't accept these small gestures without any assurances. I wrestled with the crazy notion that if I put on enough clothes, and had a good line with me, I could wander out there and find Stan. A lifetime of experience with blizzards became a myth, a fallacy. I convinced myself I could overcome the odds. Because it was Stan, dammit. Surely if anyone was meant to go on living, it was Stan.

I couldn't even begin to think about going to bed. When I wasn't pacing around the kitchen, I stood at the back window, trying to come up with a solution. Or trying to burn up the energy that drove me toward the door. I watched the snow with complete focus, looking for the smallest sign that it would let up. And each time I imagined a letup, I grabbed my coat, ready to push outside. But each time, the snow came back harder.

Muriel was also up, but we were like strangers waiting for a train. We performed our own vigils, pacing across the room from each other. Or sitting quietly. We didn't talk.

Finally, in the deepest darkness of that horrible night, the worst night since I'd watched my sister Katie die of spinal meningitis years before, or fished my nephew George from the reservoir, Rita shuffled from the bedroom and wrapped herself around me. I was too preoccupied to pull away. The snow had not let up.

"You have to come to bed," she said. "You've got to get some sleep."

"I can't."

"There's nothing you can do."

"The snow could let up any minute."

"Go to bed, Blake," Muriel said. "I'll wake you up if it breaks."

"You're the one who should sleep."

Muriel raised her brow, shaking her head. "Do you honestly think I could fall asleep?"

Predictably, neither Muriel nor I slept. Nor did we ever talk, though we occasionally shared red-rimmed glances. Finally, just as the sun peeked over the Three Hills, the storm broke. The wind didn't stop, but it slowed, and the snow fell with a soft, drifting lilt. I grabbed my coat and rushed for the back door.

"Be careful, Blake," Muriel called.

Outside, the world was like a great porcelain fairy tale. The sunlight brought pastel shadows to the icy covering, and the wind had polished the surface to a hard crust. But the crust was thin, breaking with every step. I sank to my knees, and between the freezing air and the struggle to wade through the snow, I gasped for breath.

I slogged first to the grain elevator, and it took me five minutes to make the one-hundred-yard journey. The quiet inside the elevator was magnified by what it told me. My calls echoed, followed by nothing. I moved on to the shop with the same result. The next stop was the barn, a long walk. The effort it took to push through the snow wore me down. My thighs burned. My chest burned even worse. The icy air crept in and wrapped around my lungs.

I searched the barn even though I got no response to my calls. I pictured Stan huddled somewhere, so cold that he couldn't answer. But the only signs of life were the horses and the milk cow, who asked with her eyes why I would leave without doing my job.

From the barn, I tried the next obvious choice, knocking on Bob and Helen's door. I was too tired and worried to be concerned about dealing with Helen, but I was still relieved when Bob answered.

"What's wrong?" he asked.

I cleared my throat. "Have you seen Stan?"

"Stan?" He shook his head. "What happened?"

"He was out looking for the kids when the storm hit last night."

"Are the kids all right?"

I nodded.

Bob's mouth turned down. "Well damn. Let me get my coat. I'll help you look."

"No, you don't have to..."

He gave me an annoyed look. "I'll be right back."

I didn't fight, but I heard low mutterings from inside. There was a brief rise in Helen's voice but it quickly receded. When Bob came back, she followed behind him. "Is there anything I can do? Is Muriel okay?"

"That's okay, Helen. It's real nice of you to offer though."

"Well, let me know if there's anything you need."

"We should hurry."

"Yes," Bob agreed, and at the same time, Helen said, "Of course. You'll find him. I'm sure you will."

I nodded.

But my hope dwindled as we forced our way through the snow, which became wet and heavy as the sun warmed.

"Where'd you look so far?"

After I told him, he asked, "What about the chicken coop?"

I stopped. "Wow. I didn't even think of it." I started a slow slog. Bob eased past, with fresh legs and a good night's sleep. The wind had blown directly toward the chicken coop door, and the snow drifted almost to the top of the frame. We pushed the door open, but we had to scoop away half the drift just to clear enough room to kneel down and ease through the doorway. The chickens protested in loud, strutting fashion, insisting that we leave at once.

Against the south wall, Stan sat with the wide-eyed expression of someone who'd just witnessed the most brutal of crimes. He was onion white, with a hint of blue. Ice hung from the brim of his hat, from his ear lobes, and his nose. His arms were wrapped around his knees, which were folded against his chest. I knelt at his side and put a finger to his neck.

"Oh my god," I muttered.

"He's still alive?" Bob asked under his breath.

"He is."

We didn't have to discuss a single move, crouching on either side, wedging our hands behind and under him. We lifted, each of us with one arm behind his back and the other beneath his knees. His joints didn't give, which scared the hell out of me. He was a human statue. We had to set him gently on the snowdrift outside the door, then climb out individually to get through the opening. Then we knelt again, scooped him up, and started a maddening trek through the deep snow. The sun now shone, and the snow had softened enough to feel heavy as mud. Bob and I worked along sideways, sometimes stumbling, sometimes losing our grip. I couldn't tell which were more tired—my arms or my legs.

"You okay over there?" I asked.

Stan moaned, although it was more like a croak—barely audible. My muscles suddenly felt stronger, and Bob got his second wind, too. We moved faster, with authority, stepping in unison—right foot, left foot, right foot, left foot. Twenty yards from the house, we started yelling.

"Rita! Muriel! Oscar!" we repeated the names until the back door burst open and the three of them came running. Muriel led, and when she reached us, she threw her arms around her husband, crying his name. The tears leaked from the corners of her eyes.

Rita held Muriel from behind. "Is he alive?"

"He's alive," I announced. "Somebody start warming up some water, we're going to need to get him in the tub. We need to get him warmed up."

"We already did," Rita said.

"Oh my God, he's alive," Muriel said, her voice breathy. "I can't believe it."

She held his face in her hands, feeling it as if she'd never been so close to a real person before. "He's so cold, Blake."

"I know, Muriel…we're gonna have to be very careful. You guys need to start rubbing some snow on his hands and his face."

"Snow?"

"Yeah, we need to ease his temperature down slow. Take off his gloves and rub his hands and face with snow."

Muriel tugged at one glove, and Oscar grabbed the other.

"Can't make the water too hot or it'll put him in shock," Bob said.

"That's right," Rita agreed. "Let me go add some cold water."

Stan moaned, and Muriel embraced him, making our progress difficult. Bob tripped.

"We have to get him to the house, Muriel," I said.

"Oh, I know. I'm sorry." She stepped to one side and began rubbing snow on his blue skin.

Oscar held the door open, and we slowly worked our way through, having to tip Stan to get his long legs through the door. We rocked our way through the house to the bathroom, where Rita dumped a bucket of cold water into the tub. She buried her hand in the water.

"Let me get one more bucket of cold water," she said. "It's still a bit too warm, I think."

"There's no hurry," I said. "We don't want to put him in for a few minutes anyway. Muriel, why don't you fill that bucket with snow."

We lowered Stan to the floor, and I removed his coat while Bob pulled off his boots. I unbuttoned his shirt. Bob loosened his belt and trousers, and pulled them to his ankles. When we had him stripped to his underwear, we rubbed snow on his feet, his hands, and his face. We waited for fifteen minutes, allowing his temperature to rise gradually while Rita continued to adjust the bath. After rubbing him with snow, we ran cold washcloths over his skin. Muriel wrapped herself around him when we weren't doctoring him.

When Stan's color started to come back, Bob and I lifted then lowered him into the tub. Stan's body tensed, and began to shiver. Was it too soon? A shuddering moan escaped his throat. His jaw dropped wide open. His vacant look became surprised.

"Is he okay?" Muriel asked.

"Yeah. He's fine. It's natural," I said, but I really didn't know.

Stan's toes were purple; he'd clearly suffered severe frostbite. Except for his lips, which were bright blue, his body was the color of a baby mouse—transparent pink. His joints remained rigid as we scooped cups of water over his shoulders and back. Muriel took a rag and repeatedly soaked it in warm water, rubbing it all over his face and neck. Stan continued to shiver, but red splotches appeared. Color slowly seeped into his face.

"Has anyone called the doc?" I asked.

"I did." Rita dumped a bucket of warm water into the tub. "He said to do just what we're doing, and then get him to bed...keep a close eye on him."

"God, I'm so glad he stayed inside the building," I said.

"It's a miracle, really," Bob said. "You know it must have been tempting as hell to try and find the house."

We all hummed our agreement, then fell into a grateful silence.

Stan's color returned a little at a time. Although his eyes were open, he stared vacantly, and his muscles continued to twitch. After a half hour in the bath, warming the water bucket by bucket, we lifted him from the tub, dried him off and eased him, still folded, onto the bed. Muriel pulled the covers to his neck then crawled onto the bed beside him. She scooted along the mattress and pasted herself against his back. The rest of us left the room just as she put her cheek against his.

Then we all collapsed in the living room. After a few minutes, the lack of sleep and the exertion caught up with me in an instant. My body was one big ache. Rita sat next to me, leaning her head against my shoulder.

"Do you think he's going to be all right?" she asked.

"I wish I knew."

"He looked so scary."

I nodded, but my mind went blank as sleep descended.

Oscar spoke from across the room. "I saw a man freeze up worse than this a few years ago. Got caught in a storm like last night, only he was out in a pasture. He pulled through. Lost a few toes, but he's still alive."

"His feet looked bad," Rita said. "Do you think he'll lose some toes?"

"Could be," Oscar said. "Better than freezing to death, though."

"That's pretty obvious," Bob muttered.

Oscar was smiling, but it quickly faded. He slapped his palms against his thighs. "I guess I better get out there and feed those cattle."

"Let me get my coat," I said.

"You're wearing your coat," Rita said. "Besides, you're not going anywhere, mister."

"No, he needs help with the feeding. With this storm, there's gonna be some work to do."

"I'll give him a hand," Bob offered.

Oscar turned to him. "You sure? What about yours?"

"You can give me a hand with those, if you don't mind."

Oscar looked at me, as if he wanted to make sure I approved. I wanted to argue, but I was practically asleep already. "You guys go on," I said. "Don't kill each other out there."

They both shot me a look, then started to leave the house.

"Thanks for your help, Bob," I said.

He waved without looking back.

"That should be interesting," Rita said.

"That should be very interesting."

"Let me tuck you into bed, cowboy." Rita stood, and held out her hand. I took it, and she pulled me up.

"Can you keep an eye on him?" I asked.

"Well, Muriel's got it under control right now, but of course, Blake. I'll check in on him."

As Rita held me up, one arm around my waist, leading me to our bedroom, it hit me that just a few hours before, I thought for sure we'd lost Stan. And now he slept, just on the other side of the wall. How different our lives would be if we'd found him dead. How different this moment would be, grieving and arranging. How different our futures would be. I realized how much I would have missed what Stan brings to our little family, and with the fatigue and the emotion of the morning rubbing against my nerves like the wind outside, I broke. Tears burst from my eyes. Rita stopped, turning to face me. And she wrapped me in her arms.

Chapter 8

Stumbling into the living room at four o'clock four mornings later, I found Stan sitting in front of a fire, his bandaged foot, three toes lighter, propped up on a stool.

"You're up early," I said.

His mouth curled on one side. "Actually, I'm up late."

"Your foot hurts that bad?"

Stan shook his head. "No, it's not too bad. Just worried about work."

"Ah. Well hopefully this will break soon, so you can get back there and set things straight."

"Ha." Stan's laugh lacked its usual gusto, but it still made me smile. "I was listening to the radio. It's forty below out there."

"Another hot day."

"Planes are dropping food for some of the families that are stranded."

"That's good," I said. "I'm sure there's a bunch of 'em out there."

"Be careful, Blake."

"I will." I looked out the front window, where the snow piled halfway up the pane. "I heard they lost three hundred head of cattle the other day at the Hash Knife, in one coulee."

"And you guys have only lost how many so far?"

"Just a handful, thanks to Oscar."

"He's something, isn't he?"

As if on cue, Oscar appeared, rubbing his knuckles into his skull.

"Good morning, Oscar," Stan said.

"Is it still winter?" Oscar asked.

It took three weeks after Stan nearly died before the weather cleared up enough for him and Muriel to return home. The impact of the storm took even longer than that to sink into our conscience. Ranchers in our county had lost hundreds of cattle and sheep, many of which were buried alive when they tried to find shelter from the wind. Bob had lost ten head in a draw in the Three Hills Pasture.

At least seven people died, either freezing to death, or in one case, starving when they ran out of food. The phone lines went down for several days, leaving some people completely shut off from the rest of the world. On top of that, the storm had caused untold thousands of dollars in damage to equipment, buildings, and bodies. Stan was not the only one to lose toes to frostbite.

On the other hand, the snow brought the promise of a big spring runoff, which meant another good year for hay. Which meant better feed for the stock. Which meant another good year. Our fortune seemed to be growing on itself, cycling back with increasing speed. Even this soon to be legendary storm brought some good news.

Dad could not get used to this. His distrust of success was too well ingrained—too much a part of him. He shook his head each time we bought something remotely extravagant.

"That old separator was perfectly fine."

"Yeah, but it's twenty-five years old, and this new one will save Rita a lot of time. With the baby coming, we need to think about these things."

"Your mother had babies up to her ears, and she got by with the old one."

Sometimes there was just no point in arguing.

By the time March rolled around, the snow melted away, revealing the dead gray grass. The stock celebrated, munching as if they hadn't eaten all winter. Oscar and I spent a week setting up the lambing tents. We had about 1500 head of ewes, so we set up 300 tents, which gave the pasture the look of a Hooverville for sheep.

Our mood was colored by promise. The sheep had weathered the winter. The grass flowed thick. The sky was huge, and blue as denim. And to top it all off, the long rest had worked wonders on Dad's health. He insisted on giving us a hand.

But the work was brutal. We often had to chase a ewe on foot before wrestling them to the ground and carrying them into a tent. Dad couldn't do that, so I spent most days on foot while he rode through the flock, pointing out the ewes that were about to drop.

"You got that mama over there?" I asked, watching a ewe wander toward the southeast corner of the pasture.

"Yeah, I'll get her." Dad spurred Mulie, who trotted toward the ewe. He looked better in the saddle than he had in several years. The time he spent in bed had allowed his back to heal up. He no longer slumped, trying to ease the pressure. His legs responded to each canter with a slight bounce at the knees.

About the time Dad reached the ewe, I heard a faint sound from behind. I turned. In the distance, a figure rode toward us, the horse galloping. I ran over to Mouse and climbed into the saddle, riding toward the horseman. As we closed the gap, I could see that it was Oscar. Because he was so good with horses, I knew that he wouldn't be pushing Patsy so hard unless he had a reason. I spurred Mouse. Oscar was yelling, but I couldn't hear him until we were twenty yards apart.

"It's Rita!" he announced.

"Is she okay?"

"She's having the baby!"

"Oh god." I buried my heels into Mouse's flanks.

"You want me to take over here?" Oscar shouted.

"Yes," I yelled over my shoulder.

I rode Mouse as hard as I dared—so hard that my thighs were sore from holding myself up by the time I covered the mile back to the house. I swung from the saddle, tied Mouse to the hitching post, and raced inside.

"Where is she?" I asked.

"Blake?" Margie Glasser emerged from the bedroom.

"How's she doing?"

"She's doing great, Blake. The doc is on his way, and she's doing just great."

"It's so early though. She's not due."

"Don't worry." Margie put a hand on my forearm. "Lots of babies are born early. She'll be fine."

"Can I go in?"

"Just for a few minutes. She needs to rest up for the big push."

"'Course."

I crept into our bedroom, where they had drawn the shades. Rita lay under the blankets, propped up against the headboard. She had braided her dark hair, and tied the braids on top of her head. Sweat gathered in beads along her hairline. She wore her favorite nightgown, white cotton with blue roses. She smiled, but her eyes looked tired.

"Hello, sweetheart," she said.

"How you holdin' up?"

"Good. I think I'm ready."

"Ready for what?"

Rita's mouth turned up. "I'm too tired to come up with anything." Then she grimaced.

I approached the bed. "You okay?"

"A contraction. Maybe you should go make some coffee."

"You want some coffee?"

Margie had just entered the room, and she chuckled.

"No, knucklehead," Rita said. "It's for you."

"Oh, right." I leaned over the bed and kissed her forehead. "Let me know if you need anything."

She blew me a strained kiss as I left the room.

For the next several hours, I wore out the floorboards, smoked my tongue dry, and drank coffee until I shook like an engine out of tune. I played solitaire until the nerves in my fingertips grew tender. The doctor showed up an hour later and ducked into the bedroom. I saw no sign of him after that. So I was left alone to ponder my future.

From the bedroom, I occasionally heard Rita's moan or cry, and each time, it made me want to rush in and do something. After all, I did know a few things about delivery.

By the time Dad and Oscar came in from lambing, turning the duties over to Ole Stenhjem, our night man, I had walked four or five miles, all in two rooms. They sat with me for a while, and we played cards and talked about everything except what was happening ten yards away. Finally, when Dad was too worn out to stay up any longer, Oscar looked across the table at me, over his spectacles.

"How you doing there, Blake?"

"I'm good…fine."

"Yeah?"

"Really. I'm good."

Oscar shook his head. "Boy, if I was in your shoes, I'd be a wreck. I'd be pounding pillows or something."

"Yeah…well, I guess I am a little nervous."

Oscar just smiled, his blue eyes twinkling behind his dusty glasses.

We heard a groan from the bedroom, and this one grew to a scream. I stood.

"I think I should go in there."

"That's probably not a good idea," Oscar said.

"Yeah…you're right." But I remained standing, and a long, sustained moan echoed from within the bedroom, followed by a hard, strained squeal. "I should go in there."

"You want to go for a walk?" Oscar suggested. "Some fresh air might be good."

"Yeah. Okay."

But just as we reached the door, Margie emerged from the bedroom. "Where are you going, Blake?"

"We were just going to take a little walk…is everything all right?"

"Everything's great…you got yourself a little boy."

"I do?"

"Can't you hear him?"

Then I did hear him—a faint whimper. But seconds later a full wail burst from the bedroom. I rushed in to see Rita surrounded by pillows. Her head rested against the headboard, tilted to one side. She looked exhausted, but she also had the calmest, most serene grin. Lying on her abdomen, wrapped tightly in a tiny cotton blanket, was my son. The bundle was topped with a patch of thick, black, matted hair.

I approached, standing as close to the bed as I could, bent over Rita, and kissed her temple. And I looked down at the unfocused stare of my baby boy, gazing out into the blurred unknown.

Chapter 9

One evening around suppertime, Oscar and I drove back from Belle Fourche, where we'd spent the day picking up supplies, including a new carburetor for the tractor. The sun filled the western sky, reflecting pink off a low, soft bank of clouds. It had been a frustrating day as neither of the implement companies had the right part. The last one referred us to some guy outside of town, and it took us almost an hour to find his house.

Rita had also given me a grocery list as long as an evening shadow. So we'd spent another couple of hours at the store, roaming the aisles. I expected we'd get home mid-afternoon, and I was anxious to get back to my wife and my son Benjamin.

"What do we got goin' on tomorrow?" Oscar asked.

I stared out the window, studying the thick grass, and thinking about the last time everything was this lush.

"Blake?"

"Hm?"

"What are we doing tomorrow? The shearing crew doesn't come this week, do they?"

"Nope…next."

"Are you okay?" Oscar pushed his glasses up his nose.

"Yeah. Why?"

"Just seem distracted."

"Sorry. Just thinking."

Oscar nodded. "Can I ask you something?"

I frowned, smiling. "Of course."

Oscar blushed, a rarity. "What's it like, looking down at a little piece of yourself like that? Havin' your own kid."

I shook my head. "Everything feels like it matters a little bit more, I guess. Like it's all leading toward something."

Oscar looked thoughtful. "I'm gonna have to find another wife," he announced, peering through those foggy lenses.

"All right." I nodded. "You got anyone in mind?"

Oscar looked out the window.

"Ah ha…you do, don't you? Who is it?"

"I don't think you know her."

"I doubt that, considering there's about five single women in Carter County."

"Well, she lives in Belle."

"Oh, so do you know her from when you worked for Tabor?"

Oscar nodded.

"We should have looked her up. Why didn't you say something?"

"Well, I did see her, actually."

"Today?"

He nodded.

"Where?"

"She works at the market."

I chuckled. "You sly dog. Holding out on me like that. That gal that took our money?"

Oscar's face turned a shade of red that seemed dangerous to his health. I knew which girl he meant. She was pretty, with curly black hair and a single dimple. Always friendly. Now that I thought about it, she was especially friendly that day.

"Well well." I reached over and shoved Oscar's shoulder. "I can't believe you never mentioned this. We could have stuck around for a few minutes so you could talk to her."

"Well..." Oscar cleared his throat, turning his face to the window.

"Well what?"

He cleared his throat again. "I've never talked to her, so I wouldn't have a lot to say."

I wanted to laugh, but Oscar's embarrassment was so evident that I held back. "You know her name?"

He shook his head.

"How long have you had your eye on her, Oscar?"

"I s'pose it's been a few years now."

"Oh boy...we need to do something about this."

Oscar turned away, and the back of his neck flared as red as a campfire. "I guess that's up to me. If anybody's gonna do something, it oughta be me."

"Oh no. If you've been thinking about this girl for several years, and you don't even know her damn name yet, there's no chance I'm leaving this up to you."

Now Oscar clammed up tight. So we rode the fifteen miles from Alzada in silence.

Pulling into the drive, I was surprised to see Rita walking in from the barn, carrying a bucket. Since Benjamin's birth, I had not seen her without him attached to some part of her. As soon as I parked, I jumped out and ran to her.

"What's wrong?"

Rita chuckled. "Nothing's wrong. I just decided to do the milking. I wanted to get out of the house for a few minutes."

"Okay."

"I have done this before, you know." She hooked her hand in my elbow.

"I do remember."

She kissed my cheek. "I've never seen you worry so much."

"Well hell, sweetheart..." I wagged my head, not really sure how to even respond. "Who's watching him?"

"Dad."

"Oh, jesus. He doesn't even know which end to diaper."

We entered the house and stopped abruptly to see Bob sitting at the table, nursing a cup of coffee. Dad sat fast asleep in his chair. Before I got a chance to ask, Bob piped up.

"Dad called and said the baby was crying."

Rita laughed. "They do that, all right. Looks like you got him under control."

"Well, Helen did."

Rita and I exchanged a quick glance, then moved as one toward the bedroom, trying not to be obvious.

The bedroom door was open and the first thing we saw was Helen's back, lying on the bed, curled up, hunched over. The scene, her pose...it all looked wrong, in ways too frightening to even absorb. Rita screamed, "Helen!"

Helen jumped and her head jerked toward us. "Oh, my goodness, you scared me half to death. I didn't hear you come in."

She propped herself up with an elbow, and Benjamin appeared beneath her. Rita practically dove over Helen, snatching Benjamin from the mattress and clutching him close. I stood next to her, studying my son. The sudden motion had startled Benjamin and he cried for a short while. We saw no obvious marks, nothing unusual, but his face was too pink for my liking. Helen stood.

"Dad is asleep," she said. "He fell asleep as soon as we got here."

Neither of us seemed capable of speaking. Helen started playing with her hair. "He just conked right out." She snapped her fingers. "So anyway, I guess we should probably be getting home."

Rita and I stared at each other with dumb shock. My mind had the vague idea that we should thank Helen for watching Benjamin, but I couldn't seem to move the thought from my mind to my tongue. Helen didn't seem to expect anything anyway.

"I'd just let him sleep." Then Helen left the room, and we heard her and Bob talking on their way back to their house. We simply stood looking at each other, with Rita silently snuggling our little boy against her shoulder.

"What do you think she was doing?" Rita poked a needle through the thick denim of a pair of my dungarees, patching a hole in the knee. Benjamin lay nestled in his bed, Dad was still asleep in his chair, and Oscar had gone to bed.

"I don't want to think about it." I turned back to my newspaper.

Rita shook her head. "I hate thinking that about anyone, especially someone so close to home."

I pushed my lips up toward my nose, taking off my reading glasses. "I know what you mean."

"But I do." She looked surprised at her own admission.

I could only nod.

"Are you sleepy?" she asked.

"I was just thinking about turning in."

Rita set the dungarees to one side. "I think I'll join you."

We milled around, putting away dishes and feeding one last log to the fire, before I wandered over to Dad's chair and gave him a nudge.

"Time for bed, old man." But his shoulder felt hard. There was no give. He didn't respond. "Dad?" I gripped his upper arm, which also felt too hard. "Dad?"

"What is it?" Rita moved toward us, already bending at the waist.

"Damn!" I shook him, grabbing his shoulders. "Dad! Wake up."

"Blake." Rita spoke gently, placing a hand against Dad's cheek.

My chin fell to my chest.

Rita's hand moved slowly down his face until it rested on his shoulder. I sank onto the armrest and Rita sat on the other one. We both sat looking at him for a while.

"He looks peaceful, doesn't he?" she said.

I nodded. I felt a tear trickle down my cheek.

"Look." Rita held up a cup, then looked inside it.

We sat quietly for a long time. But after again looking into the cup she held in her lap, a slight change came over Rita's expression, a realization. "Blake."

"What?"

"Blake, she said he fell asleep right after they got here."

"So?"

"Hot chocolate takes a long time."

"Oh come on, Rita."

"Blake." She fixed a look on me. "What do you think she was doing to our boy?"

"Rita, she's not one of my favorite people, but that doesn't mean I believe she's going to come into our house and start killing people."

"And what if she did, Blake?"

"Rita, please." I sat on the stool at my father's feet. "My father is dead. Can we not talk about Helen right now? Please?"

She sighed and sat on my lap. Her arms looped around me, loose and tired. And she cried a little while we held each other. "I'm sorry, Blake."

"It's okay."

"But she did this. I just know it."

Chapter 10

I wrapped a navy blue necktie around my upturned collar and flipped one end over the outstretched length of fabric.

"Are you ready for this?" Rita asked.

"I can think of quite a few places I'd rather be right now."

"You and me both." Rita held a black pillbox hat like a layer cake, and set it carefully on top of her head. She plucked a bobby pin from her mouth, and pried it open with her teeth.

Thirty feet away, in the living room, sat my father's casket, its lid closed for good to hide the effect of a very thorough autopsy. A few neighbors prepared food in our kitchen, and Pastor Ludke dozed in Dad's chair. We could hear more guests arriving. Margie was watching Benjamin, which gave us this rare moment alone.

"You told Buddy not to come, right?" Rita asked.

"Yes, I remembered."

"Good. I just know he'd say something."

I nodded. "I agree."

Although I fought it hard, I finally agreed to have someone look into the circumstances of my father's death. But to initiate an investigation, we had to go through Buddy Walters, the sheriff of Carter County and a second cousin of our late neighbor, Art. Behind his back, people ridiculed Buddy for being inept, but his obvious weaknesses always seemed to be more a matter of inexperience. Not that he was very smart.

When we talked to him about our suspicions, he said, "You know that would be a murder, right, if she did what you're saying she did?"

"Uh…yes, Buddy. We do realize that."

He nodded thoughtfully. "Just wanted to make sure."

Buddy agreed to arrange the autopsy. It would take several weeks to get the results.

I donned my suit jacket, then turned to see Rita putting the last touches on her lipstick. "Shall we?" I asked.

She took a deep breath. "I'm ready if you are."

I thought I was ready. But I lost my breath when I opened that door into our living room. Near the front, in a black suit so shiny and smooth it looked polished, my brother Jack rolled a cigarette with one hand.

"Hello Blake." He spoke as if he'd been gone a day or two.

I could barely manage a nod and a handshake.

"How've you been?" Again, his tone was so casual, so conversational, that it rubbed up against me like a muddy dog.

"I need to say hello to some of the guests."

Before I had a chance to turn away, I felt a presence next to my elbow, and a hiss burned my ear. "Do you have any idea at all how unwelcome you are here?"

I watched my brother's mouth curl into an unnatural, tight smile. "Hello, Rita."

"What are you doing here?" Rita's voice was low, and quiet, but it simmered with hatred.

"My father died," Jack said.

"Well, you sure sound busted up about it," I muttered.

The front door swung open, and Bob and Helen entered, her cheeks already moist with tears. She held a handkerchief against one side of her eye.

"Hello, Bob…Helen." Jack reached for Bob's hand.

I felt Rita disappear and I also turned away, losing myself in the crowd. Pastor Ludke conducted a brief service. Just as my father had always wanted it. No church, no fanfare, no fuss. I hardly heard a word anyone said the whole day. I looked right into peoples' eyes and heard nothing but a blurred murmur of muddled consonants. Fortunately, their words held little mystery. If anyone sought answers to crucial questions, they didn't let on. I nodded, and thanked everyone for coming. And I kept Helen in the periphery of my vision, especially if she drifted anywhere near our bedroom where people took turns watching Benjamin. I held my other eye on Jack, giving myself a headache when they crossed paths.

I watched Jack corner Teddy for a half an hour and overheard him tell him he should come and watch Captain Andy race sometime.

Stan and Muriel had driven down from Butte, and it wasn't until Stan pulled me aside after the service that I finally managed to relax a little. Stan collared me in the kitchen, taking my hand and shaking it with both of his. "Blake, what can I do? Anything. Just tell me."

I chewed the inside of my lip. "Well, if I think of anything…"

"Absolutely. Anything." He continued shaking my hand. "Now tell me something, Blake." He finally let go. "What's this crazy rumor…"

I panicked. Rita and I had been very careful to keep our suspicions about Helen to ourselves, and we'd given Buddy specific instructions to do the same.

"What are you talking about?"

"I heard Jack is coming back to the ranch."

I grabbed the front of Stan's shirt, gathering it in my fist. "Stan, that's not one bit funny."

Stan opened his mouth, holding his palms out. "I'm not kidding, Blake. That's what I heard."

"Who did you hear that from?"

"Your brother." Stan shook his head. "I'm sorry. I just figured you knew."

I guess there are two ways you can look at the fact that I didn't believe what my sister-in-law was up to until that moment. You could say that I trust people too much…that I tend to give people the benefit of the doubt. That my belief in human nature is optimistic to a fault. Or you could say that I'm not too bright. It really doesn't matter. What matters is that at that moment I realized that we were about to get ambushed. That my wife's warnings carried real weight. That while I plugged through my days, trying to make a life for myself and my family, others had designs to take that life away. With methods and plans and manipulations that were beyond my comprehension.

I knew that Helen was capable of anything. But until that day, I really believed that Rita and I had built a solid shield against whatever schemes she might cook up. That we would somehow be immune to that evil by our simple devotion to doing the right thing.

Without thinking, I stalked across the room and told Bob that we needed to talk. The look he gave me told me everything. I slammed our bedroom door shut. When I turned, Bob looked as if he'd been in the bed with pneumonia for a week.

"Did you offer Jack a job?"

"Why?"

"Because I heard that he's coming back."

"Why would I even have to? He's part of the family. He can come back here any time he wants."

"So is he coming back?"

"Why don't you ask him?"

"Because I'm asking you." Without realizing it, I had eased my way so close to Bob that I was breathing on him.

"What if I did? Is it only okay for *you* to hire people without asking? This is not your damn ranch, Blake. There are other people involved in this place, you know."

I stopped. I took a deep breath. I pointed at my brother, nearly poking him right in the eye. "How important is it to you that we keep this family together, Bob?"

He dropped his eyes with a confused, almost stricken look, as if this subject had never once crossed his mind.

"How far is your wife willing to go?" I asked.

The door suddenly opened and, as if on cue, Helen appeared, apple cheeked and innocent. "Bob, honey, do you want something to drink?" She acted as if I wasn't in the room, looking at her husband with the most loving expression.

"Not right now."

"I'm not interrupting anything, am I?"

"Yes you are," I said.

"Oh really." She said this with indignation, almost mocking me, and I came to my second frightening realization of the day. I saw in Helen's face, and heard in her voice, that the mutual respect I had always imagined was just that...completely imagined. It wasn't there at all. This woman hated me with a contempt I had never felt from another person. And at that moment, I felt exactly the same way about her.

"Yes, really."

"Perhaps this is a conversation I should be part of." She turned from me to Bob.

"I think we're through here," Bob muttered.

"Only for the moment," I said.

"And just what exactly is it that's not over?" Helen asked, her smile still sticky sweet.

"I think you know the answer to that better than anyone in this room," I said.

Chapter 11

We didn't see any sign of Jack for a couple of weeks after the funeral. I wasn't about to ask whether he was coming. Bob began to devote more time to his own cattle. We'd get an early morning call from Helen, saying that Bob would be too busy to cut the hay that day, or that Bob had to run to town and get some more feed. So Oscar spent more time on the tractor.

On the days that Oscar and I worked together, I tried not to think about Bob and Helen by plotting a strategy for Oscar's friend at the market. He managed to speak to her once—a simple 'hello.' I could tell by the way her dimple burrowed into her cheek that it charmed her.

On our next trip to town, we discussed a plan.

"You need to know exactly what you're going to say, before you even go inside the building. Otherwise, your brain will freeze up like ice cream. So all you gotta do is start by asking her name. Nothing complicated."

"Okay." Oscar cleared his throat, pushing a knuckle to his glasses.

"And then you say, 'nice to meet you, so and so…my name is Oscar, and I wondered if you'd be interested in going to the dance in Alzada this Saturday night.'"

He nodded. "All right. I think I can manage that. No more than two lines, though, or I'll forget."

"You want me to write it down?"

"Shut up," he said, laughing.

"Just trying to help."

A half hour later, walking along the sidewalk to the market, Oscar muttered to himself, trying to clean the hay dust from his glasses, coughing while he practiced. As we approached the market, we came upon a paper sack lying on its side. Oscar took a deep breath and planted a swift kick into the heart of the sack. The sack flew into the air, but as it began floating back to earth, two objects continued the path of flight. One of them was a half-eaten apple, which soared ten feet past the sack. The other landed short of the apple and began shaking itself. Then the black and white figure crouched into a stance, its fluffy tail pointing straight in the air. And a misty cloud rose up and swallowed us.

We both shouted, raising our hands and backing away. The skunk waddled away, off-kilter from the kick. Shoppers heard the commotion and rushed outside, and I could vaguely see the outline of a crowd gathering. My eyes burned, and the spray stung my face and hands. Moisture ran down my cheeks as my eyes tried to wash away the spray.

Slowly, the scene came into view. Oscar stood with his legs far apart, his arms dangling away from his body. I started laughing. And I couldn't stop. Oscar took off his glasses, rubbing them against his shirt. I was surprised he wasn't also laughing until a glance to one side revealed that the girl of his dreams stood a few feet away, covering her mouth.

"What are we gonna do?" Oscar asked.

And this just made me laugh harder.

"Do you guys need some clothes?" the girl asked, and the act of speaking released her laughter.

"That would be very helpful," I answered while Oscar stared at her.

"Are you okay?" she asked him.

"What's your name?"

Her smile got wider. "Georgia. Why?"

"Nice to meet you, Georgia. Would you like to go to the dance in Alzada this Saturday night?"

There was a short, awkward pause. "Are you going to wear that perfume?"

"Only if you like it."

Georgia's smile spread. "I'd love to go."

At this point, Oscar seemed to lose all of his senses. He smiled at Georgia for a few seconds, then he started walking toward the market.

"Um…Oscar," I called.

He turned. "Yeah?"

"You probably don't want to go in there."

He looked down at himself, as if he just remembered what happened. "Yeah. Right." He staggered back toward me, and Georgia's hand clamped hard over her mouth again. The crowd began to drift, holding their noses.

"I'll get some clothes for you guys," Georgia said.

"Let me give you some money," I said.

"No, it's okay. We don't want to stink up the cash register."

"Oh yeah. Well, you can put it on my account then."

"Arbuckle, right?"

I smiled. "Very good."

Oscar and I moved further from the market, isolating ourselves from people. We couldn't even stand too close to each other, the smell was so bad.

"You did it, buddy," I said.

"I did, didn't I?" Oscar chuckled. "How did I do that?"

"Don't forget to find out where she lives."

A panic came across his face. "How am I gonna pick her up?"

"You'll use my car, of course."

"Can I?"

I shook my head. "You damn fool. You think I'm gonna help you get this far and then make you ride Patsy?"

Georgia rounded the corner, carrying a bundle of clothes. Then she stopped, looking at us with her mouth pulled to one side. "If I give these to you, you'll just stink them up before you even get a chance to put them on. You guys need to take a bath."

"Where are we gonna take a bath?" Oscar asked.

"I have an idea," I said.

"I guess I should come with you," Georgia said.

"Will they let you leave?" I asked.

"I think they will…considering…" She turned on her heel, then tossed one more comment over one shoulder. "I'll get some tomato juice, too."

Georgia set a case of tomato juice on the sidewalk, where I retrieved it. She then followed twenty yards behind us with the bundle of denim. Oscar was still too nervous to talk, so I took on that burden.

"Did you grow up here, Georgia?"

"Sure did. Born right here in Belle."

"Who're your folks?"

"Bill and Sheila Barnes."

"Oh really? I know your dad real well from REA. Tell him hello for me."

"I'll do that, Mr. Arbuckle. I know he's talked about you. That's why I knew who you were."

"You can leave out the skunk part if you want." I winked.

"Oh but that's the best part!" she said, laughing.

The conversation continued in its odd manner, with me shouting over one shoulder while Georgia shouted from behind.

"Your name's Oscar?" she yelled.

"Yes, ma'am."

"Most people tell you their last name when you ask them their name," Georgia said.

"Sure they do," Oscar agreed. "MacArthur."

"Oscar MacArthur?"

"That's right."

Georgia chuckled.

"What's so funny?" Oscar asked, clearly charmed.

"It's a good name," she said. "It's like a nursery rhyme or something."

"That's good?" Oscar asked.

"Sure it is. Who wouldn't want their name in a nursery rhyme? I sure would."

I couldn't help but laugh.

"Are you laughing at me, Mr. Arbuckle?"

"Of course not, Georgia. I'd never do such a thing."

"Better not," she instructed.

Oscar's smile could not have been wider.

I led them to the local livery stable where we approached a young kid pitching hay into the stalls. He grabbed his nose.

"Sorry to impose our stink on you, young fella, but we could use your help," I said.

"What do you mean?"

"We need to take a bath."

He studied us, still pinching his nostrils. "You want to take a bath here?"

"Yeah, I thought you might have a water trough

you're not using, or even a stall with a bucket...something like that. We can't go in anyone's house, you see."

"Yeah." He made no move to further the discussion.

"So you think you can set us up with something? We'll pay, of course." We stood in our little cloud of skunk odor, with Georgia ten yards to one side.

"I need to ask the boss."

I looked around the stable, and saw no sign of another person.

"Okay...well...where's your boss?"

"He's at home."

I looked at Oscar, who covered his mouth.

"Okay...well, is his house far from here?"

"No, not far."

The kid stood there.

"Well, do you want me to go ask him?"

"No. I better do that." He dropped his pitchfork and sauntered down the street.

Oscar, Georgia and I looked at each other and immediately burst out laughing. I set the case of tomato juice on the ground.

"You think the smell got to him?" Georgia asked.

"It was infecting his brain," Oscar said.

"Georgia, you don't have to wait around. You can just leave those."

"Well, what if he says no?" she argued. "I'll wait until he gets back."

"That's real nice of you," I said.

"Yeah, well, don't get used to it," she said.

So we sat on the rail and Georgia sat on her own, close enough to talk. We chatted for five minutes and Oscar even spoke up a few times. Georgia blushed, smiling, and stared at him each time he spoke.

"Oscar, are you going to ask me where I live so you can pick me up Saturday?"

"Of course. I was just about to do that." Oscar made a dramatic show of clearing his throat. "Georgia, would you mind telling me where you live so I can pick you up this Saturday?"

Georgia giggled.

I took a little walk to give them some time alone. I realized that I wasn't going to be able to make one of the stops I had planned for this trip. I wanted to stop in at the bank and check on the ranch account. On top of everything else, I could just imagine that Helen had figured out some way to get her hands on the ranch money. Not for the first time, either. The stable boy returned a few minutes later, walking as if he had all the time in the world.

"So what did he say?"

"Huh?" He looked up, staring at me. I honestly think he had no idea who I was. He covered his nose.

"What did your boss say?"

"Oh…he said it's okay."

"Great. So we can use one of the troughs?"

"Yeah. He said you can."

"Okay. Do you want some money?"

"No, that's all right."

"Well thank you very much."

We bid farewell to Georgia and stripped in one of the back stalls, where the kid helped fill the trough with water he heated on the wood stove. We took turns bathing, soaking in the tomato juice, scrubbing our skin raw. After bathing for an hour, we were covered with red patches, and we still smelled like spoiled cabbage. We couldn't scrub any more without rubbing off a layer of skin, so we crawled into the stiff new clothes, and burned the old ones in the stove, throwing foul smoke into the air. The day had seeped into late afternoon and we hadn't eaten since breakfast.

I turned to Oscar. "Let's go see if we can get thrown out of the café."

It was dark by the time we approached the house that evening. When we came up over the hill, I saw a car parked in front of the house. I thought it might be Jack, but as we pulled into the drive, I recognized Buddy Walters' patrol car. This surprised me, as he said it would be six weeks before we heard anything about the autopsy results.

Oscar and I entered and Buddy and Rita rose from the table. I felt the same pang that tugged at me each time I walked into the house and saw Dad's big chair empty.

"What's that smell?" Rita asked.

"Oh, we had a little argument with a skunk," I said. "How you doing, Buddy? Don't worry about shaking my hand."

Buddy nodded, tugging at his belt. "I'm doing all right, Blake. Good to see ya."

I turned to Oscar. "Oscar, would you mind excusing us? You want to take a bath?"

"Actually, Blake..." Buddy pulled his belt up toward his ribs. "I need to talk to Oscar."

I stopped in the middle of whatever I was doing. "Oh?"

Buddy cleared his throat. "Yeah, I actually came out here to arrest one Oscar MacArthur."

"What?" Oscar looked at me, then back to Buddy. "What for?"

"Well, Mrs. Arbuckle has accused Oscar MacArthur with stealing some money."

I looked at Rita. "Not me," she said.

"Sorry," Buddy said. "Mrs. Bob Arbuckle. Helen."

"God *damn* her," I slammed a hand against the table. Then I pointed at Buddy. "Buddy, you know damn well…" But I stopped myself.

"Blake, I'm sorry. I gotta do my job," he said.

Once I found out that I couldn't bail Oscar out until the next morning, Buddy cuffed Oscar and led him off to the car, and Rita and I sat dejected in the dining room.

I shook my head. "The baby's asleep already?"

Rita nodded. "Speaking of sleep, do you think she sleeps over there? Do you think she's sitting up right now thinking of something else she can do to mess with our lives?"

I sighed, letting a loud puff of air escape. "You gotta wonder."

Although Oscar was never charged with anything, Helen's actions had the desired effect. As if she had taken our thumbs and tightened the screw to them one more rotation. From that day forward, I often found myself staring out the window at Bob and Helen's house, as if a torpedo might suddenly burst from one of the windows and come whistling toward us. It was the same for Rita, and occasionally we would have to remind each other to tear our eyes away.

And the most irritating part was that she knew it. From that day forward, whenever we had the misfortune of seeing them, the look she gave us told us that she knew. And every time I saw that look, I became more and more afraid that there was nothing we could do to stop her.

Chapter 12

That Saturday Rita and I put on our weekend duds and prepared to make the fifteen mile-drive to Alzada. It was a clear night, and quiet like it gets only in the prairie. There were almost no sounds as we walked to the car. Oscar had just finished cutting the hay in the Hay Creek Meadow, the smell as sweet as canned plums. Rita held a slumbering Benjamin, his little body wrapped tightly in a red cotton blanket, close to her chest.

"I sure hope Oscar has a good time," Rita said.

"You and me both."

I had been very concerned about Oscar's report of his night in the Carter County Jail. He said Buddy asked him no questions.

"It felt like I was there to keep him company," Oscar said. "He talked my ear off before his deputy came."

It did not bode well, relying on someone like Buddy to find out what happened to my father.

I tried my damnedest to put those annoyances out of my head and enjoy myself for the evening. I took my time driving, inhaling the clean spring air. Benjamin stirred a few times but didn't make a sound. We shared several of the goofy smiles that new parents sometimes do, the kind that say, 'Can you believe we made this thing?' I had the window cracked and could almost smell the grass growing. The air was as fresh and sweet as new milk, and it rushed through the car like a child on Christmas morning.

We approached Alzada, which consisted of about thirty buildings, and pulled into the parking lot of the town hall, the social center of every small town in Montana. Because we had waited for Benjamin to fall asleep, we were later than usual, and a large crowd had already gathered.

We ducked inside and were immediately surrounded by folks who had not yet seen the baby. They said all the right things and Rita's cheeks glowed. Benjamin played his part perfectly, sucking at the air in his sleep.

Oscar and Georgia shuffled across the dance floor, which made me happy. Although Oscar had tagged along to several dances since his arrival, I had yet to see him raise any sawdust. I could now see why, as he was a truly horrible dancer. With his thick arm wrapped tentatively around Georgia's waist, he rocked back and forth like a crippled hobby horse. But he didn't seem the least bit embarrassed, or even aware. He was having a good old time, and Georgia's smile, spread like fresh honey, indicated the same.

When I caught Rita's eye, I tilted my head toward them and she smiled. "Aren't they adorable?"

"They look pretty good together," I agreed.

"It would be so nice to see him find a nice girl after what he's been through."

The comment was overheard by a couple of Rita's friends, who wanted to know what she was talking about. When Rita started to explain, I wandered off to chat with some people. I was pleased to see Steve Glasser, wearing a bright green shirt. I joined him at the table, where he was talking to John Birnham, a distant neighbor.

"What's the story?" I asked.

"We're just trying to decide who's the worst dancer out there," John said.

"Not much of a contest, is it?" I said.

They both laughed. "So far…no," Steve agreed.

"Well, I don't see either of you out there…you afraid of looking even worse?"

"I know I would," John said.

"I'd give you a run for your money," Steve added.

"Well, as long as you're wearing that shirt, nobody's gonna care how you dance," I said.

"Are you going to be able to dance with the baby here?" Steve asked.

"We'll just set him up at the bar."

I considered asking Steve how he was holding up, but I knew this wasn't the time. So the conversation followed the predictable path of crops and cattle. When the band eased into the early strains of "Tennessee Waltz," one of Rita's favorites, I excused myself. When she saw me coming, Rita handed Benjamin to one of her friends.

"Shall we?" I asked.

We swayed and swirled, and the song pulled us around the floor. Perfumes mingled with the smells of sweat and cigarettes and booze, and boots scraped along the sawdust-covered floor. We worked our way over to Oscar, and I winked at him. He peered over his glasses, which had steamed up like a winter window. He blushed as if he'd been caught at something.

Bob and Helen showed up about an hour later and from the minute they entered, it looked as if they were in the middle of a fight. Bob went one way, heading for Steve's table. Helen, who carried a plate of sandwiches, ducked into the kitchen.

Rita nuzzled up against my ear as we two-stepped to "String of Pearls."

For the next hour, while the band guided us through every mood swing imaginable, a second dance played out around the edges of the dance floor. Bob, Steve and John Birnham sat huddled at the table, and Helen went nowhere near her husband. I had my eye on Oscar and Georgia, and whenever they got anywhere near Bob's table, I felt my shoulders get tight.

"Blake, what's wrong?" Rita asked about the third time this happened.

"Nothing," I said.

She leaned forward, her mouth close to my ear. "I know you better than that."

"I just don't want anything to spoil Oscar's night," I said.

Rita looked over her shoulder, then smiled at me. "I think Oscar's doing just fine."

Just then, Bob, Steve and John left the building, and I did a quick scan of the dance floor. When I saw Oscar and Georgia shuffling along the far end, I relaxed a little. I held Rita close, and the band started up with "Who's Sorry Now?"

As the evening wore on with no sign of unpleasantness, Rita and I wore out the dance floor. My son cooperated by sleeping blissfully through most of the evening, even as our friends passed him around like a birthday gift.

Bob and Helen apparently made up, but always deftly avoiding us. Around one o'clock, Rita told me she was tired and we started gathering our stuff. I ducked into the kitchen, looking for one last bite of sandwich, when I heard a strange murmur pass through the crowd, followed by a loud but short exclamation.

"No, please," I said.

When I made my way back out to the dance floor, the cause of the commotion was not what I expected.

My brother Jack stood in the doorway, red-faced and smiling, his arm around a woman I'd never seen before. He held his hat out in one hand, like a performer, his hair plastered against his forehead like paint. A few people approached to greet him, but most of the crowd turned away from the door and went back to what they were doing.

"I heard there was a dance," Jack shouted.

Just as if they were just waiting for someone to verify this, the band kicked into a new song. I pushed through the crowd to Rita, who gathered the last of our things. I kept an eye on Jack, hoping they would move away from the door.

"You ready?" I asked.

"More than ever."

I glanced toward the door, happy to see that Jack had moved, until I saw him walking directly toward us.

"Blake!" he shouted, as if a great friendship had suddenly developed between us. "Come on, Tina. I want you to meet my brother Blake." He pulled his date by the hand. She stumbled, and I couldn't tell who was drunker.

"How you doin', Blake?" Jack reached to shake my hand, and I took it with as little enthusiasm as possible. He wore the same suit he wore to Dad's funeral, although it didn't look nearly as neat.

"Can we go now?" Rita asked.

"We're just leaving, Jack," I said.

"Well that's not very nice," Tina whined, smiling.

"Yeah…well, we got a little one here. We need to get him home to bed," I said.

"Well, will you look at that." Tina tripped toward Rita, who looked as if she was about to punch her. Tina leaned over Benjamin, and Rita turned a shoulder toward her.

"Whose baby is that?" Jack asked.

"We need to get going," I said, taking Rita's hand.

"Jack, you never told me you had a little niece," Tina said. "Look how cute she is."

"It's a boy," Rita snapped. "And we really need to leave."

Tina stepped back. "I'm sorry," she muttered. "He's just so cute, I thought…"

"It's okay," Rita said. "I know you didn't mean anything by it."

"Gotta wonder whose baby that is." Jack's bleary gaze stared somewhere near my head.

"I don't think we need to wonder about that too much, Jack. Now it's real late, and we're tired."

Jack nodded, and his gaze moved slowly to Rita. The dance had become so crowded that we were wedged in--the only way out was around Jack.

"Excuse me, Jack." I took Rita's hand, and started to ease past him.

"Of course, little brother."

"Nice to meet you, Tina," I said.

"Sure didn't seem that way," Tina complained.

"Good to see you, Rita." Jack's tone made me want to choke him, but I clamped my jaw and led Rita away from the scene as quickly as the crowd would allow.

Driving home, we sat silent for a time. Finally, Rita shook her head.

"That poor woman must think we are the rudest people to walk the earth."

I chuckled. "Hell, she was so drunk, she probably doesn't even remember meeting us."

Rita nodded. "That's probably true." She looked down at Benjamin. "Blake, do you ever feel like there are some mistakes you make that will just never go away?"

"Aw, sweetheart, you were just a kid. You didn't

know." I reached out and rested a hand on her arm. "Besides, did you ever think that it might have been part of my plan to get you out here?"

Rita smiled. "Oh Blake. What a lovely thought. Of course that's why it all happened."

"See?" I smiled at her.

But she looked out the window, pausing for a long, silent moment before saying, "God, why won't he just go away?"

Chapter 13

A few days later, coming in for supper, I was surprised to find Teddy sitting at the dining room table. He rarely came to visit in the middle of the week.

"What's goin' on?" I asked.

"Jenny's coming home tomorrow," he explained.

"That's great," I said. "Isn't it?"

Teddy nodded. "I hope so."

"Well, she must be doing better if they're letting her come home, right?" Rita said.

Teddy shrugged. "I really don't know. Margie doesn't like to talk about it too much."

Jenny had been hospitalized for six months, and we'd heard talk that she might not come home at all.

"Well, let's just hope she's doing better," Rita said. "Do you think they'd mind if we came by tomorrow evening, or should we wait?"

"I think it would be a little early, but I'll let you know," Teddy said.

"Please do," Rita said.

"So what are you doing here?" I asked.

"Well, Steve and Margie went to get her, and…"

"He came for the food," Rita said.

Teddy grinned, blushing.

For the next two days, Oscar and I bent our backs to one of the more grueling and mundane jobs of ranch life. We still had the bulldozer that Jack left behind when he disappeared, and Bob had decided to build a small dike along the southwest corner of the Hay Creek Meadow, to capture a little more runoff. But it needed some finishing work and that meant shovels. Digging.

Oscar and I strained wordlessly, battling the earth. Since the drought had broken, water soaked into the clay and silt so that a small shovel filled with gumbo weighed as much as wet cement. The grass roots sank deep into the mud, grabbing each wedge of soil, pulling back when we tried to pry it from its home. The earth smelled moist and alive.

I switched arms every half hour to keep from wrenching my back. But the burn stretched along one side until it settled deep into my muscles. When I switched, I would feel strong for a few minutes. By the end of the day, I could barely stand up straight. But Oscar shoveled in a steady rhythm hour after hour, showing no sign of fatigue.

"When are you gonna see Georgia again?" I asked on the drive home.

He smiled. "Saturday."

I nodded. "Glad to hear it."

The sun was just visible above the peak of the house.

"I didn't realize how late it is. No wonder I'm tired," I said.

"Hell, I should have reminded you an hour ago then." Oscar winked.

As we parked and climbed from the car, headlights appeared just over the rise a mile up the road. Walking toward the house, I watched the vehicle approach. "I wonder if that's Jenny."

"Did Steve go to pick her up?"

"Yeah."

But an unfamiliar pickup appeared in the dusk, pulling a horse trailer. The pickup was brand new, shiny black, and barely coated with dust. It pulled into our drive.

"This doesn't look like somebody looking for work," I said.

"No it doesn't." Oscar stuffed his hands in his pockets and turned for the house. "But just for the record, I'm not planning on leaving."

"Thanks for clearing that up."

As Oscar went inside, the driver stepped from the cab. The sun shone in my eyes, but in the fading light, he bore the same look as many of the drifters from the thirties, with a long, craggy face, deeply lined, and a hat pulled down over his eyes. We walked slowly toward each other.

"Howdy, Blake."

I looked up. "Ah. So it's true."

Jack reached out to shake. "Good to see you."

We shook hands. "How are you doing, Jack?"

"Never better."

"Is that Captain Andy back there?" I jerked a thumb toward the trailer.

He breathed in deep. "Matter of fact..."

I nodded. "That's one hell of a horse."

Jack puffed himself up. "He's a treasure." He nodded, agreeing with himself, looking out over the ranch, the place where we'd shared our entire history. He pulled his hat off and scratched the top of his head.

"So where's Tina?"

Jack chuckled, shaking his head. "Let's not talk about that."

"What brings you here, Jack?"

I remembered the last time he'd come back—standing in the same spot. That time, he'd returned with a pocketful of money, the bulldozer, and a different brand new pickup. And that was during the Depression.

"Just came by for a visit." He measured me, then winked.

"Yeah." I nodded, tilting my head. "Well, I'm guessing you're not here to visit us."

He dropped his eyes. "That's true."

"I need to get some supper." I turned and walked toward the house.

"Good to see you, Blake."

I waved over my shoulder. The house echoed with the sounds of supper preparation. Oscar was setting the table and Rita carried a plate of roast beef from the kitchen.

"What's he doing here?"

"Whoa," Oscar muttered.

"I don't know," I said.

Rita sighed, setting the roast in the middle of the table. She looked up at me with a fire in her eyes that stayed all through supper.

After we'd finished eating our chocolate cake, I went and checked out front, and the vehicle still sat there, ominous in its blackness. I finally heard the engine fire up later that evening, and I went to the window again, this time watching it slowly rock its way toward the barn. I knew Jack had gone to unload Captain Andy. He wasn't going anywhere.

This could have been the worst news we'd had in weeks, but the phone rang not too long before I trudged off to bed, and it was Buddy Walters.

"How's it going, Buddy?"

"Well, I'm doing all right," he said. "But I'm afraid I've got some news you're not going to like so much."

"Yeah? You got the results?"

"I did."

"Not what I'd hope for, huh?"

"No, 'fraid not, Blake." Just in case Buddy didn't have enough presence to not go into details on the party line, I thanked him and hung up. Then I swore.

"What now?" Rita asked.

I shook my head. "That was Buddy."

Rita grabbed my arm. "You know that's not right, Blake. We've got to do something."

I nodded, and I knew she was right. But at that moment, I didn't have it in me, and I wasn't sure when or if I ever would.

Chapter 14

Teddy stopped by the following evening, his mood considerably improved. "Jenny seems happier than I ever remember," he said as we sat down to supper.

"That's terrific," Rita said

Teddy nodded. "The last time she came home, she stayed in her room for days, and she looked like a damn ghost."

"So she looks healthy?" I asked.

"She's got color in her cheeks!" Teddy took a big bite of chicken.

"I don't remember her ever having any color," Rita said. "She's always been so pale."

"So whose pickup is that outside?" Teddy asked casually.

There was a brief silence before I answered, and he looked up. "It's your dad's."

Oscar dropped his fork. It landed with a great clatter. He recovered quickly and tried to resume eating as if it was a complete accident.

"Where is he?" Teddy asked.

"Over at Bob's," I said.

Teddy frowned. "Why isn't he here?"

"We didn't want him here," Rita said.

"How can you say that, Mom? He's still part of this family." Rita continued eating, ignoring the question. Teddy followed with another. "Did you tell him you didn't want him here?"

For a moment, the question brought a guilty silence to our table.

"Son, there are some things about this situation that might take you awhile to understand," Rita said.

"That's bull, Mom." Teddy paused. "I know the details. I was there when he accused you two of having an affair. I know he lied about the war, and took off, and all that stuff. But he's still part of the family. He built all those dikes and did a lot of good things around here. You've got no right to treat him this way."

"I agree," Oscar said firmly.

I turned to him. "This is none of your business."

"You're right, Blake. I apologize." Oscar went back to his food.

"But he's got a right to his opinion," Teddy said.

"Son, you've got a heart the size of Montana," Rita said. "But this is a family matter."

"I agree," Oscar said. "I really am sorry. It just kinda popped out."

"Well I think he should be able to express himself," Teddy insisted.

"Teddy!" Rita barked. "You will not talk to your uncle that way. Do you hear me? That is not how I raised you."

Teddy bowed his head. And I felt a strong sense of gratitude toward my wife for stepping in. I was surprised how much I took Teddy's defense of his father personally. I had spent most of the years during Jack's absence acting as a father to the boys, even living in the same house for several of those years. And although I'd never thought of myself as a substitute for Jack, thoughts of 'how dare you!' started running through my head. I had to clamp my jaw shut.

"Sorry, Ma," Teddy finally said.

"Well you should be apologizing to your uncle, not to me."

"He doesn't have to apologize to me," I said.

"Well I want to." Teddy turned to him. "I'm sorry, Uncle Blake."

"Maybe we ought to just get on with our meal." I spoke more harshly than I intended, which drew quick glances. But it got the desired effect, and the discussion stopped.

As soon as we finished supper, Teddy left without explanation and I knew he'd gone to visit his father. Again I was surprised to find myself feeling this like a thump in the chest.

A half an hour later, after we'd all settled into our places, footsteps and laughter echoed from the front porch. I swallowed my tongue as the door swung open, and Teddy led Jack through the living room, where I sat reading the *Ekalaka Eagle*. They made their way to the dining room, where Oscar was playing solitaire. While everyone said polite hellos, Teddy went into the kitchen to pour two cups of coffee.

Rita was in the bedroom nursing the baby, and I felt funny sitting alone in the living room. So I took a deep breath and joined the others at the dining room table.

"So what's everybody been up to?" Jack asked.

The question brought a predictable silence at first, but after looking around the table, Oscar spoke. "Busy. We been real busy. Between getting the first cut of hay done and digging this irrigation ditch, there's hardly been time for the stock."

"Well I'll be happy to lend a hand if you guys need some help. Just let me know." Jack buried his fingers in his hair, which had remained just as thick and dark as it had ever been while mine slowly thinned to a wisp.

"We don't need help," I said. "We're busy, but not any busier'n we've always been."

After taking a long pull from his coffee, Jack rubbed the back of his neck, tilting his head to one side. "Well, Bob said he could use a hand with his cattle, so I think maybe I'll take him up on that offer."

"What a surprise." The words jumped from my mouth without thought, the anger coloring them just as thick and dark as they felt.

"What's wrong, Blake?" Jack smiled at me.

"Well…for one thing…it seems funny to me that Bob wouldn't need help with those cattle until now."

"And what else?" Jack glared at me.

"We can't afford to pay another hand." This wasn't quite true, but that was beside the point.

"Nobody said anything about you paying me," Jack said. "I don't need the money."

I shook my head.

"Listen, this place is my home," Jack said, "and I've got the resources to help you folks out here. But I'm not here to help out of the kindness of my heart."

"We'll take your word on that," I muttered.

"All right, you got me there," Jack said. "But all I'm saying is…I can help."

"Isn't that fair?" Teddy asked.

"I wish everything was that simple," I said.

After a time, and some general chatter about the weather, Jack told everyone good night and left. Teddy also excused himself to go back to Glasser's. Rita emerged from the bedroom.

"What was that all about?" I could tell by the shape of her mouth that she could barely contain her anger.

"Jack's staying…working for Bob."

"Damn him," Rita said under her breath. "He couldn't just let us be, could he?"

I lowered my eyes. "Let's just hope he's not here long."

"Boy," Oscar said, almost to himself.

"I know." I nodded. "It probably sounds like we're a little hard on him, but…well, if you knew the whole story…"

Oscar just shook his head. "You've been saying that ever since I got here..."

I wasn't able to fall asleep that night, a problem I almost never experienced. I rolled over and over until Rita turned a tired eye to me and told me to get up if I was going to keep her awake, too. So I slipped from the bed and sat on the back porch, listening to the chirping crickets.

I wondered why on earth Jack wanted to come back here. I thought back to the day George drowned. The day that the reservoir Jack built wrapped itself around his son, forcing water into George's lungs until it smothered him, and spitting the shell of him onto the ground. I believed we'd never see Jack again after watching him attack that reservoir with a huge stone. I didn't think he'd ever be comfortable living out here in the open space, with the memory of his son, and our brother George, who also drowned, and of our sister Katie, who died after running home to tell us about discovering George's body. I thought these memories would keep Jack away.

But here he was, and I wondered again, as I had so many times, what mysterious hold this land has on its people. How can it be that a place that pummels people so thoroughly, that asks them to sacrifice everything, can still manage to take you in its arms and comfort you into thinking it's going to take care of you? What is it about this flat, expressionless expanse of dirt that tells us these lies?

I sucked the fresh, sweet, clean air into my lungs that night and thought again how much Jack and I were alike in this one respect.

But why was he here?

Chapter 15

When I came in from the fields one evening, Rita sat reading a book while a stew simmered on the stove. Benjamin dozed in his basket at her side. This was the third or fourth time I'd seen her reading in the past week, and because she rarely had time to sit down, I settled in next to her and lifted the book to see what it was.

"Hey," she scolded.

"I just want to see what's got you so distracted there."

"Oh." She looked embarrassed. Still, she held her thumb in the folds of the book and showed me the cover. The book was called *The Book of Poisons*.

I raised my eyebrows. "You learning anything?"

Rita nodded, distracted, and went back to her reading.

"What are you planning to do?" I asked.

Rita lowered her chin and looked at me from the top of her eyes. "What do you think, Blake?"

"You think you're going to figure out how she did it?"

Rita's hands dropped to her lap. "Blake, would you rather just sit around and wonder for the rest of our lives?"

I sighed, looking across the room at my father's empty chair. The tractor needed a new fuel pump, the fence along the south side of the Three Hills pasture was badly in need of repair, there seemed to be an outbreak of scours among our yearlings, which meant we needed to vaccinate sometime very soon. And Mouse needed new shoes.

As good as Oscar was, he and I were only two men. And now that Bob was devoting more time to his own stock, the work had piled up. I missed my father.

"Don't you want to know what happened?" Rita asked.

I laid my head back. "But we *do* know what happened. What difference is it going to make?"

Rita suddenly sat forward, leaning her elbow on her knee. "Blake Arbuckle, I will not sit by and watch you do this."

I frowned. "Do what?"

"You're giving up, and I'm not going to allow you to do that."

I closed my eyes.

She spoke quietly. "I miss him too, you know."

I nodded, leaning my head against her shoulder. "I think we need to hire another hand," I said.

"I wondered how long it was going to take you to admit that."

The next evening, Rita and I bundled up Benjamin and drove to Glassers for a visit. Since Jenny's return, we'd been over there once for a brief chat. But there were several other people there, and it was apparent from the minute we walked in that the attention overwhelmed Jenny.

Rita had called every day since, giving me a report each time. The day before, Rita thought she sounded a little 'funny.' "Like she was about to fall asleep. She kept trailing off in the middle of her sentences."

We drove the two miles to Glasser's with a quiet drizzle tickling the roof of the car. Benjamin complained, but he wasn't really crying. He'd been fighting a cold for a week so we hadn't had a good night's sleep for a few days. Rita stuck a knuckle in his mouth, and he moaned his way through the unhappiness. When we pulled up over the hill a hundred yards from the Glasser place, Rita and I groaned at the same time. Bob's '45 Chevy sat in the driveway.

"Should we come back another time?" I asked. "I know you're tired."

Rita didn't answer right away. She sighed. "We really need to see her."

"We can leave if it gets awkward."

She nodded. "I'll give you a sign."

"I don't think I'll need one," I said.

Steve looked surprised to see us and glanced behind him as we entered. But he stepped to one side.

"Come on in." He shook my hand. "I guess it's Arbuckle night here. How you all doin'?"

"We're good," I said.

"How's that little fella?" Steve poked his nose near Benjamin's face, and Benjamin whimpered.

"You might not want to get too close," Rita said. "He's been fighting a bug."

"I think he's about ready to help out with the docking," I said. "He could wrestle a lamb or two, don't you think?"

Steve nodded, smiling.

We entered the living room where Jack sat across the room from Bob and Helen. Jenny perched on the sofa, a half-smile curling her lip. She looked stuffed, with her cheeks slightly puffy. Her neck looked full. Her hands lay folded demurely in her lap, a handkerchief choked tightly in her right. Margie stood against one wall, looking worried. Everyone but Jenny had a glass in their hand. We all exchanged greetings, and Bob rose from his seat on the sofa to give it up to Rita, who customarily refused before sinking into the thick cushion. Bob and I sat across the way in dining room chairs.

"Where's Teddy?" Rita asked.

"He hit the hay early," Steve said. "Had a long day."

"Is he a good hand?" Rita asked.

"'Course he is," Jack said, and a nervous laugh rounded the room.

"So how's everything going 'round here?" I asked.

"We're doing all right," Steve said. "Everything's okay."

A long pause followed, and the Glasser's generator suddenly seemed very loud.

"Anyone seen Ted Willoughby's new Plymouth?" Bob asked.

"Did he get a Plymouth?" Steve asked.

"It looks nice," I said. "I was thinking about getting one."

"Oh were you?" Rita asked playfully.

"Just thinking," I said, winking at her.

"Didn't you just buy that Ford last year?" Steve asked.

"Yes I did," I confessed. "And would you believe it already has forty thousand miles on it."

"It does not," Helen said.

I nodded. "Amazing, huh?"

"How in the hell..." Jack started.

"I think I've spent more time in Belle this year than I have in the past ten years combined," I said. "Plus just driving around the place to look things over. There's a hole in the seat already."

"I've been to town more this year, too," Bob said.

"It's the price of progress, isn't it?" Rita said.

"Yes it is," Helen agreed.

Jenny had not spoken since we said hello, and I couldn't help but notice that she still had the same tired smile. I remembered Teddy's enthusiasm after she'd been home a few days, and I had a bad feeling that his optimism had colored his view of the situation. She still looked very pale and distracted.

"I'm sorry, I just realized that we didn't offer you guys anything, Blake and Rita," Steve said. "You want something to drink?"

"I'll take some more of this," Jack said, holding up his glass.

"You have lemonade?" I asked.

"Yes we do." Steve stood.

"I'll get it, Dad." Margie started toward the kitchen, holding up a palm to her father.

"That's okay, honey. Why don't you sit down for a while? You've been standing all day. Rita, what about you? Lemonade?"

"That sounds just perfect," Rita said. "Let me help you out."

Steve motioned for her to stay put as he retrieved Jack's glass and made his way to the kitchen. "How about you, Bob? Helen?"

They both said they were fine. Margie didn't sit as Steve fixed the drinks, but she did move from that wall to the one closer to her mother.

"You hear those prices this morning?" I asked Bob.

He nodded. "Sure did."

"Prices are down?" Jack asked.

"Hell no," I said.

"They've been up for a couple years now, Jack."

I watched Jack absorb this information.

Steve returned with the drinks, his long fingers wrapped around three glasses. "What's going on with that horse of yours?" he asked Jack. "You ever gonna race that thing again?"

"Funny you should ask." Jack accepted the glass from Steve, and I could smell the whiskey. "He's going to be running next weekend, up at Capital."

"I'd like to go to that," Jenny said suddenly.

Jack sat up straighter. "You would?"

Jenny smiled. "Yes I would. I'd like to see the horse races."

"Well, I'm not sure if that's...." Steve said.

Standing behind her mother, Margie was shaking her head vigorously.

"No, Steve," Jenny said. "I really think it would be nice. I'd love to see a horse race. I can't remember the last time."

Steve sighed. "Well okay, honey. Maybe we'll do that."

Margie dropped her head into her hand, shaking it slightly.

"I think it would be very good for me to get out and do something like that," Jenny said.

"I agree with you one hundred percent," Jack said.

"Well if you guys go, we'll go," Rita said, much to my surprise.

"You will?" Now Jack was almost standing. "That would be great."

"I'm not sure I'll be able to get away that day," I said.

"Sure you can, Blake," Jack said. "You're practically the damn boss there now. You can get out for a Saturday afternoon."

I wanted to say something about how being the boss made it that much harder to get away, but Rita gave me a look, and I could just tell that she had something different in mind than I did. I knew I better go along or I would hear about it later.

"We'll see," I said.

"Hey, this is gonna be great!" Jack said.

Outside, Bob, Helen, Jack, Rita and I walked toward our vehicles. All of our heads were down except for Jack, who was beaming, staring up at the stars.

"What a gorgeous night," he exclaimed.

"It sure is," Helen echoed, making a distracted glance of her own.

"See you folks in the morning," I said as we climbed into the car.

As we pulled onto the main road, Rita turned to me. "I think we should go to support Jenny," she said.

I nodded. "I figured that out eventually."

"Okay."

Benjamin suddenly woke up, crying loudly, and

Rita struggled with her garments before giving him a breast. "What do you think is going to happen to her?" I asked.

"She'll never make it," she answered without the slightest hesitation.

"God, I wish it wasn't true, but I agree with you."

Chapter 16

That Sunday we drove the twenty miles to Capital, where Captain Andy was scheduled for the fifth race of the day.

Jack had been up early. He spent the morning taking Captain Andy out for an easy run, then feeding and grooming him. Teddy came by to help his father, then they left around nine o'clock.

The crowd, larger than I expected, piled into the small Capital rodeo grandstand. As we climbed toward Steve, Margie, and Jenny, who were sitting near the top, we heard a buzz about whether Texas Wind would run. A rumor spread that he was injured.

We settled in behind the Glassers and said our hellos.

"How's everybody doing?" Steve turned, and his skewed eye wandered off to the side.

"We're doin' well," I said. "How about you folks?"

"Great," Steve said.

Jenny sat with a big smile, although she didn't appear to be looking at anything in particular.

When they led the horses out for the fifth race, most of the crowd searched for Texas Wind. The rumors had shifted and changed all afternoon about his leg—everything from a small cut to certainty that he'd been put down. A murmur shivered through the crowd when his familiar dusty brown coat moved with its easy stride in the middle of the row of horses. But in our little group, the attention was focused on Captain Andy.

"Oh no," Rita said.

"What's wrong?" I asked.

"Look at the jockey." She pointed.

"What the hell…"

I was shocked to realize that the lanky figure perched atop Captain Andy that sunny fall afternoon was my nephew Teddy, his legs folded up like a grasshopper's.

"Did you know Teddy was riding?" Steve asked.

"We had no idea," I answered.

"Teddy's riding?" Jenny had been sitting with that unfocused smile, and her body turned with her head toward the track. We all looked at Margie.

"I didn't know, either," she said.

A light dust drifted as the horses made their way toward the gates. I watched Rita's anticipation grow as the horses walked in a slow circle behind the gates.

"Is Teddy going to be okay?" Jenny asked.

"He'll be fine, darlin'," Steve answered.

A look from Rita told me that she shared Jenny's concern. I laid a palm on her arm.

There were seven horses in the race. Much like the race in Ekalaka, Captain Andy looked out of place among them, like a beaver coat in a pile of burlap. I watched Jack give last minute instructions to Teddy. At first, Teddy nodded with an attentive expression, but it eventually became clear that he didn't want to hear any more. He kept repeating 'okay' over and over. But Jack kept talking, gesturing decisively. He didn't stop until the horses had ducked into the gates. My nephew adopted the ready position, crouching into Captain Andy's neck.

"I'm worried," Jenny said.

The bell sounded. The horses broke, and Captain Andy surged forward, moving a length, then two lengths, then three lengths in front of the nearest horse. By the time he reached the first turn, Captain Andy had settled into a coast. He led by nearly ten lengths. Everyone in our little group stood, yelling like our lives were at stake—even Rita.

Texas Wind's jockey led him into the middle of the pack. But it became clear from the beginning that the other horses did not share the fluid grace of the leader. They rounded the track once, and Captain Andy lengthened his lead. On the second lap, hitting the far turn, Texas Wind pulled ahead of the rest of the pack. But Captain Andy was so far ahead that he could have walked. He came out of the final turn with Texas Wind halfway down the backstretch. Texas Wind's jockey pulled out his whip, and his right arm went to work, pumping away at the horse's flank. Texas Wind responded, churning forward.

He edged further away from the third place horse. While Captain Andy skimmed the surface of the track like a water bug, Texas Wind's hooves burrowed into it like a plow, throwing clumps of dirt behind him. Captain Andy crossed the finish line with a whoosh, and as Texas Wind and the third place horse entered the stretch, Texas Wind led by a neck. But two other horses were gaining ground, easing up along the rail.

Texas Wind worked that final one hundred yards like a new pair of gloves, clenching and uncoiling, rolling forward. One horse that he'd battled for half the race pulled forward in the last few yards, and the one just behind him also snuck up along the rail, his nose lining up with that of the other horse just as all three of them crossed the finish line. It was impossible to tell whether Texas Wind had finished second, third, or fourth.

Our little cluster of fans clapped and looked at each other with a combination of joy and surprise.

"What a race," Rita kept repeating.

"Wasn't that wonderful?" Jenny said.

Jack ran onto the track, taking Captain Andy's reins. As Teddy climbed down, Jack pounded him on the back.

"How long until they announce the winners?" Steve asked.

"Did we win?" Jenny said.

"How much did you bet on him, Blake?" Oscar asked.

"Oh, I don't bet on the horses," I said.

"Not even today?"

"Never have been much of a gambler. How much did you bet?"

"Hell, I'm not gonna tell," Oscar said. "Then I'd have to share."

"Did we win?" Jenny turned a confused smile from one face to another, then another.

"We did, Mom." Margie wrapped an arm around Jenny's waist.

"Ladies and gentlemen, we have the results of race number five." The announcer's voice echoed through the grandstands, and everyone was suddenly quiet. "The winning horse is Captain Andy. Placing was Panama Lucy, and to show…"

A small group of people just to our left erupted, and we didn't hear who finished third.

"What did we win?" Jenny asked.

"Jack's horse came in first place," Steve explained.

"Then why are those people there cheering?" Jenny asked, pointing to the other crowd.

"Second place is very good in horse racing," Margie said. "They still win money."

"Oh, is it?" Jenny turned around where she was standing, so that she was facing us. "How was I supposed to know that?"

"Nobody expected you to know, Jenny," Rita said.

"It's just so hard to remember everything." She turned back toward the front.

Rita handed Benjamin to me, climbed down next to Jenny, and wrapped an arm around her. "I know, Jenny. It's okay."

Steve glanced at me and then turned toward the track, and even in that brief bit of eye contact, I saw a sad display of helplessness. He began to climb slowly down the grandstands, as if his escape might not be noticed if he walked without making any sound. I decided I ought to go congratulate Teddy. And Jack. So I caught up to Steve.

"Great race, huh?" I said.

"It was. I figured he'd win, but I didn't expect that."

"I don't suppose anyone did."

"Amazing…" I said.

Steve nodded and fixed his good eye on me. "It is."

We reached the grounds and headed toward the stables. Captain Andy remained on the track, surrounded by fans. Being that close to the horse, I was surprised to see how impressive he looked. Even after spending weeks around him, I had failed to appreciate the magnificence of this animal. His hide showed every crease in his muscles, especially in his flanks.

"Damn," Steve muttered.

I just nodded.

After that brief pause, we approached Jack and Teddy, who were combing and washing him down. Both wore smiles as wide as their heads.

"Congratulations!" Steve shouted.

"Heyyyyyyyy." Jack laid down his sponge, and we shook, soaping up our hands. "Wasn't that something? Did you see how this kid rode?"

Teddy blushed as Jack threw an arm around his shoulders. "Well, he did most of the work." Teddy jerked a thumb toward Captain Andy.

I was ashamed at how much I envied this show of affection between my brother and his son.

"You looked like a real natural up there, Teddy," Steve said.

Captain Andy tossed his head and snorted, as if annoyed by the shift of attention from him.

Behind us, a whoop echoed through the stables, and a tight, muscled fist rose up above the stalls. Oscar's smiling face appeared, his glasses perched a bit precariously, and fogged over. He held a stack of bills.

"How much did you bet?" Steve asked.

"Well, I took a little chance," Oscar said.

"You better tell me you bet on this horse?" Jack tilted his head toward Captain Andy.

"Maybe a little."

"You didn't bet a quinella on those two, did you?" Jack asked.

Oscar turned crimson, looking down.

"Hot damn!" Jack exclaimed. "What did it pay?"

I could tell that Oscar wanted to say, but that he also didn't want to say.

"Must've been about five bucks, huh?" Steve guessed.

"A little more," Oscar admitted.

"You gonna bet on the next race?" Jack asked.

"Hell no." Oscar looked at him like he was nuts. "Why would I do that?"

"Double your money, buddy." Jack slapped the back of his right hand across his left palm.

"How do you feel, Teddy?" I watched my nephew sink into the background, combing Captain Andy's neck.

"A little sore," he said. "Not used to stretching these muscles." He ran his hand down the back of his thigh.

"He made it look like he's been doing it for years, didn't he?" Jack slapped Teddy on the back. "I have a feeling this isn't the last time we're going to see these two cross the finish line in the money."

This brought a very subtle look of surprise to Teddy's face.

"Isn't that right, son?" Jack's palm smacked against Teddy's back one more time.

"Stop hitting me, Dad," Teddy said. My jaw clenched. It was not my place to say anything, and I wouldn't, but since Jack's return to the ranch, I had been wrestling with his decision to pursue this profession. Horse racing and rodeoing had always been sources of conflict when it came to life on a ranch. Because they required time and resources that were already in short supply, and usually for very little gain. In Jack's case, I didn't really care as long as he wasn't working for me, but the idea of Jack taking Teddy away from my friend Steve for any time at all, when things were already a struggle, brought some heat to my blood.

"All right, son." Jack, undaunted, clapped a hand around Teddy's neck. "Whatever you say, buddy."

I'd had as much of Jack's little show of fatherly pride as I could take. "Well congratulations again, you two. I'm gonna see what everyone else is up to."

Jack didn't even hear me, but Teddy gave a small wave. Steve came along, and as we climbed back up into the stands, I saw Jenny searching the crowd, her face twisted with worry and fear. When she saw her husband, she lit up. And at that same moment, Steve's shoulders dipped a few inches.

"If there's anything I can do, Steve," I said, but he turned and looked at me as if I'd just asked him for a thousand dollars.

Chapter 17

As I watched the railroad crew load the last of our yearlings onto the train, I tugged my best grey felt cowboy hat onto my head.

"You ready?"

I turned to Teddy, who wore a brand new suit. We had spent the last two days moving fifty head of our cattle and forty of Glasser's to Belle Fourche. I was still a little saddle sore. "I think so. You?"

He nodded once. "Yep." But a look of confusion curled his brow. "Is that Dad?"

I turned, and sure enough, my older brother strode along the platform. He smiled when he saw us, and waved.

"What are you doing here?" I asked.

"I'm going to Denver."

"Why?" The question exploded from me.

"There's a big race down there."

"Did you know we were going down for the sale?" Teddy asked.

"Of course," Jack replied.

I turned away.

I usually love train rides and I tried to concentrate on the scenery as we spent the next two days trundling through Wyoming. But despite the fact that he sat in a different car, Jack's presence lingered in the background like a bad smell. I couldn't help but think about how much work needed to be done back home. One of us should be there, and if I'd known Jack was planning the trip, I would have asked Teddy to handle the sale of our cattle. We stopped several times and Teddy checked on Glasser's cattle while I wandered through ours.

To my relief, Teddy was quiet for most of the trip.

Just a few miles out of Denver, Jack finally came and sat next to Teddy.

"So you want to ride this ol' nag in the race?"

"You don't have a jockey lined up already?" Teddy asked.

"Nope."

"What's our schedule like?" Teddy asked me.

"It's up to you, buddy," I said "You're not working for me, remember?"

"That's right," Jack said, to my annoyance.

"When's the race?" Teddy asked.

"Saturday afternoon."

"Okay," Teddy said.

I was not happy to hear this. I had been looking forward to spending some time alone with Teddy.

"You should come along," Jack said.

I turned toward the window, pretending to be dozing, although I knew I wasn't fooling either of them.

We arrived in Denver early Friday morning and went directly to the auction yards, where the big sale would start the next morning. After one last check on the cattle, Teddy and I took a taxi to our hotel, ate some dinner and laid down for a nap. But only moments after I'd drifted off, a sharp knock lifted me like a spring from my mattress. The door swung open before either of us responded, and Jack breezed into the room.

"Teddy, you ready to go work this horse for a few hours?"

"Dad, I was sleeping."

"Sorry, buddy, but we got work to do."

Teddy gored his eyes with his knuckles. "All right." He swung his legs off the bed. "All right."

I laid back, covering my eyes. "How about supper?" I asked.

"We'll just eat at the track," Jack said.

I hmmed.

I didn't wake up until several hours later, and even then, I felt sleepy. I dragged myself downstairs to the hotel restaurant for supper, called Rita, and then sat in the lobby reading the newspaper. This was one of my favorite parts of going to a bigger city…being able to read a newspaper that came out that day. I also took pleasure in watching the variety of people parading through the building. Just about the time I planned to get up and go to bed, a couple blew in like a strong wind, the force of their presence and the level of their conversation drawing all eyes to the door.

She was one of the most beautiful women I've ever seen, a statuesque brunette wearing a tailored sky blue business suit. A round little hat balanced on top of a swirl of hair, and her eyes were exactly the same color as her outfit. Her companion's hair was slick with oil, folded like a book to one side. His hair matched his shining black shoes.

"You do not tell me what to do with my life," the woman declared. "I have never been so humiliated."

The man's jaw pushed forward. "Could you please talk a little louder?" he said.

The woman stopped, then turned, looking directly at him. "What did you say?"

The man stood up straighter, but even then, he was barely taller. He raised a hand, jabbing a finger toward her face. Just as he started to say something, she swatted the hand away. The man grabbed her wrist and tried to drag her toward the elevators. She wrenched her arm free, and I stood, moving tentatively toward them.

"Do not grab me," she instructed.

He tried grabbing her anyway. Now I strode with more purpose, coming up along his side. "Maybe you should leave the lady alone," I said.

Suddenly I felt a blow to my head…not a hard knock, but enough that I threw my hand to my skull. I turned to see that she had hit me with her purse.

"What kind of person are you?" she asked, and from the expression she fixed on me, I felt a momentary inclination to come up with an answer to her question. My jaw hung loose for a second.

"Please mind your own business," she said.

"I'm very sorry," I said. "I was just trying…"

"Please…"

I thought for a minute she would hit me again, so I backed away from the scene. The elevator door opened, and they stepped inside. When the door closed, I felt the eyes of the bystanders, and I don't know whether I've ever felt so alone. As soon as the next elevator arrived, I went to my room, directly to bed. I slept so soundly, I didn't hear Teddy come in.

I rose early the next morning, and Teddy rolled out of bed as soon as he heard me stirring.

"Ready for the race?" I asked.

Teddy put a palm to his forehead. "Yeah."

"You okay?"

"I'm fine."

He turned away from me, clearly not fine. The thought that Jack would get the poor kid drunk the night before he was going to prop him on a racehorse got my blood up, but I kept my mouth shut.

Teddy didn't eat much breakfast, which further concerned me. We got to the auction yards an hour early, as I like to do. We studied the stock, although we weren't in the market to buy.

Teddy sidled up next to me. "Is it my imagination, or are our cattle huge compared to the others?"

I smiled and nodded.

We sold at a very good price, as did Teddy with Steve's. He seemed to feel better as the morning wore on.

"You gonna be okay for this race?" I asked.

"I'm good, Blake. I'm fine."

I nodded.

"Are you going to come to the race?" he asked.

"Of course…I wouldn't miss it." What I didn't say was that Rita would kill me if I wasn't there.

The grandstand was huge. I felt as if I understood for the first time what it's like to be a cow in the middle of a herd. I arrived after the races had begun, so my seat was far away from the track. I felt dizzy as I settled onto the hard wooden plank, cradling a bag of popcorn and a cup of beer.

Three races passed before Captain Andy's, and I had finished my popcorn and beer. Considering that he'd only lost one race, Captain Andy's odds surprised me...they had him near the middle of the pack. From the opening bell, it became clear that he had stepped into a new league. Captain Andy broke near the back and got boxed against the rail by three other horses.

Teddy tried to steer him between two others, jerking the reins and using his whip to push some of the horses. Halfway around the track, an opening appeared, and Teddy jumped on it. But the lead horse was far ahead. I don't think it would have mattered anyway. Maybe the trip took something out of him, but besides being overmatched, Captain Andy did not appear to be himself. He labored through the backstretch, passing a couple of horses but galloping far behind the leaders.

About the time Teddy reached the far turn, I realized that I was standing, screaming my damn head off. I had my program rolled tight in my fist, shaking that thing like I wanted to kill it.

"Go Teddy. Go Teddy. Go Teddy."

But it was hopeless. Captain Andy finished seventh, well back. I dropped my program to the ground. And I started to make my way down toward the track. Teddy and I had agreed to go out for supper after the race.

Halfway down the stands, the entire crowd gasped as one, and then started muttering to each other. I looked up just in time to see Teddy place his hands on his Jack's shoulders and throw him to the ground.

"He hit the horse," I heard somebody say.

"Who did?" I asked, not even sure whom I was asking.

"The guy on the bottom."

"Jesus." I made my way down to the grounds, but they wouldn't allow me onto the track, where Teddy still held Jack down. The cops tried to pry Teddy off him, but Teddy put up quite a fight. They finally pulled him free. Teddy's face burned red, with a long scratch running down one cheek. He was crying, and this brought angry tears to my own eyes.

Jack had propped himself up to his elbows, and a trickle of blood trailed from his nose to his chin. He looked devastated. Teddy stood over him for a moment, then turned away, and I motioned for him.

"Teddy!"

When he saw me, he dropped his eyes to his shoes.

"I'm sorry, Blake." He crawled through the fence.

"Hell, Teddy…you got nothing to apologize for."

"He hit him, Blake. He smacked the damn horse right in the head. But I shouldn't have done that."

"Well…sometimes circumstances just…you know..."

Teddy nodded, but he was clearly troubled.

"Let's get something to eat."

Jack may as well have been traveling on a different train on our way back. We caught one glimpse of him in the dining car, but he ducked out the opposite end when he saw us. Teddy was very thoughtful the whole ride. I wanted to know what was running through his head, but I held my tongue.

It wasn't until we were almost back in Belle Fourche before he turned to me with a grave expression, and chewed the inside of his cheek for a moment. "Blake?"

"Yes, sir."

"When you were living with us, when I was a kid…" He studied me, and I nodded. "…did you and my mom talk about getting married then?"

"Of course not…she was still married to your dad then."

"Yeah, I remember…but still…"

"No, we never did, Teddy."

"I wonder what she was thinking," Teddy said.

"Well…" I looked out at the flat expanse of dying grass as we passed through the last few miles of Wyoming. "Your mother is a very loyal person, you know."

Teddy scrunched his lips up against his nose. "Yeah…she is. But you know...some people don't deserve that kind of loyalty."

I nodded, feeling a swell of pride. There was more to say than I could possibly put into words.

Chapter 18

"God, these cattle look good." Stan and I stood in the back of the feed wagon, shoveling soy cake in narrow trails into the snow. The Herefords lined up behind the wagon like a red, furry stream.

"Don't they, though?"

"They're as fat as I've ever seen," Oscar said from the driver's seat.

It was Christmas morning, and Stan and Muriel had arrived the afternoon before, loaded with packages.

In the distance, we could see Jack and Bob feeding Bob's cattle.

"So what's going on with this horse of Jack's?" Stan asked. "Didn't he win a race?"

"He's won several now," I said. "He's pretty much the Joe DiMaggio of horses out here."

Stan buried his shovel into the cake, then let the cake fall in a thin stream from the shovel. "So why doesn't he go out and race him all the time?"

"Well, he's had a hard time finding a jockey."

"I thought Teddy was riding him." Stan limped across the wagon bed and shoveled from the opposite side.

"He was, but…well, they had a bit of a falling out."

Back at the house, we entered a minor battle zone. When Stan and Muriel's kids opened their gifts that morning, they'd uncovered some of the most rambunctious toys in history—cars and trains and dolls that made various noises or limped across the floor with a great clattering. Half of them were broken by the time we got back, and Dorothy had a fat lip from running smack into her mother while she was marching around playing her new tin trumpet.

"At least we won't have to hear her play for a few days," Stan whispered.

Despite all that destruction, the kids weren't worn out yet. They hovered over a board game in the living room, rolling dice and moving tiny plastic pieces along colorful squares.

After we gathered the wrapping paper and fed the fire, Stan and Muriel whipped up a batch of pancakes, and we ate ourselves into mid-day comas. We slept as if we'd never get another chance, and emerged by ones within a couple of hours, eyes puffed.

Soon the preparations started for Christmas dinner. As cooking sounds echoed through the house, I invited Oscar to join me for a drive out to deliver a plate of Christmas food and a bottle of bourbon to Ole Stenjhem, our shepherder.

Outside, the snow sparkled. The sun glowed behind the clouds like a bulb buried in cotton. Oscar and I rode wordlessly for the first half of the drive to the Washburn place, an old homestead that we'd bought in the twenties, where we wintered our sheep. Just as we approached the turnoff from the main road, Oscar turned suddenly.

"Blake, I gotta talk to you about something."

I nodded. "Okay."

Oscar turned toward the window, knuckling his glasses, then rubbing the bristles on his head. "I need to figure out how to tell Georgia about getting arrested."

"You haven't told her?"

"Mm mm." Oscar shook his head, chewing his lower lip.

"Have you even heard from Buddy since that night?"

The car rocked as we plowed through the deep snow.

"No I haven't."

"Well, I wonder if you even need to worry about it. Maybe he's not going to pursue it."

"Yeah, well…" Oscar sighed. "The thing is, Blake…well, there's more to the story than you know."

"Oh?" A mild panic passed through me.

He nodded, then turned toward the window again, staring out across the white meadows surrounding us. He was silent for a very long time. Finally, he took a deep, heavy breath, held it for several seconds, and released. "You've heard about these guys that sometimes get shipped out West because their families don't want anything to do with them, right?"

I nodded.

He turned to me, asking me with his eyes to not have to explain.

"You're one of them?"

Oscar looked down at his lap.

"What happened?"

"Well, I was just a fool is all. When I was young, I got into some trouble with the law, and my family wasn't too happy about it. Didn't fit in with their reputation, you know."

"So that whole story about your folks wasn't true?"

Oscar shook his head. "I'm sorry I lied, Blake."

"What about your wife?"

"That's true. Everything else I told you is true."

We came to a gate, and Oscar climbed out to open it. After I'd driven through, he closed the gate and ducked back inside.

"So what kind of trouble was it?" I asked.

Oscar looked sheepish now, his face filling up with pink. "Robbery."

"Oh hell."

"Yeah."

As we neared our destination, I stopped for a moment.

"Are you going to fire me?" Oscar asked.

"What?"

"Blake, I lied."

"Well, Oscar…maybe I'm crazy or naïve, but tell you the truth, that idea hadn't even entered my head."

His chin dropped. "Thank you."

"That was a long time ago," I said.

"Yeah, well…some people wouldn't see it that way."

"You're the best hand I've ever had, Oscar."

And the silence was back for a time, measured by the idling engine.

"So what do you think I should do, Blake?"

"Well, Oscar…from what I've seen, Georgia is pretty fond of you. I'm guessing she'd forgive you if you went ahead and told her."

Oscar nodded, but I could see he wasn't sure.

"Oscar, what made you bring this up? The chances of anyone finding out about that aren't exactly high, you know."

Oscar nodded. "Helen," he muttered. "She made some comment to me the other day. I think she knows."

I groaned.

Ole was taking a Christmas nap when we pulled up next to his sheepwagon. He poked his rumpled head out and waved, then emerged, tugging his suspenders up over his shoulders. He pulled on his thick sheepskin coat. Ole was well over six feet tall, with shoulders like walls and hands as big as plates. But in the twenty years he'd worked for us, I'd never seen him raise a hand to anyone. Or his voice.

"Merry Christmas, Ole." I handed him the bottle, and the plate of food, which was wrapped in a towel. Every Christmas since Ole had taken the job, we had invited him to Christmas dinner at the house, an offer he always declined.

"Is it Christmas?" Ole rubbed his eyes. "Thanks, Blake." He tucked the bottle into his pocket, then shook my hand, still holding the plate of food. "I guess I'll save my biscuits for breakfast."

"The sheep giving you any trouble?"

"Oh no."

"They got what they wanted for Christmas then?"

Ole chuckled, his rosy cheeks rising up to his eyes. Fortunately for Ole, good conversation was not one of the requirements for his job. His face looked as if it was about to blister, it was so red. As painful as it was to prolong the conversation, I had to ask him whether he needed more feed or supplies. He told me which medicines he needed after giving me a report on the ewes that were nursing ailments. An awkward pause followed.

"That supper's gonna get cold, so maybe we should stop our yapping," I said. "You hungry?"

"Well, you know I can always eat." Ole chuckled, putting a palm against his ample belly.

"Well, keep warm out here," I said.

"Will do. Thanks again, Blake."

Back at the house, thick aromas greeted us—roast beef, ham, and onions. Dishes of mashed potatoes, beets, pan gravy, and roasted carrots crowded the table. We sat down to savor the riches of our happy life. The table echoed with laughter and much teasing, and occasional scolding when one of the kids played with their food. Stan also got scolded, for talking too loud.

"How's Ole?" Rita asked.

I chuckled. "He's Ole. Didn't know it was Christmas..."

"I wish he'd join us for dinner one of these years," Rita lamented.

"It might just kill him to sit at a table with this many people."

"Especially this crowd," Stan said.

Muriel slapped his arm.

"That's not very nice, Daddy," Dorothy said.

"Sorry honey...Daddy was making a joke."

"If you're gonna make a joke, please make sure it's funny next time," I said.

"Ha!"

"Dorothy, have you ever seen a sheep wagon?" I asked.

Dorothy shook her head, her curls bouncing slightly.

"I've seen one," her older brother Hank said.

"Well, what would you think about living in one of those for a very long time?"

"How long?" Hank asked.

"Months."

Hank shrugged, but his younger brother Walter's eyes got wide. "Wow."

"Some people like it," Oscar said.

"I can see why," Rita muttered.

"You sick of us, Rita?" Stan asked.

"Just a little."

Stan winked at his kids. "You ready for some more taters, Hank?"

"Shoot no…I'm as full as a tick," Hank declared.

"Anyone else?" Stan held the potatoes at eye level, to no takers.

"What about dessert?" Rita asked. "Anyone ready for a piece of pie?"

All kid hands went up, which brought a wink from Stan. The adults also hummed their approval.

I helped Rita cut and serve three pies—pumpkin, apple, and mincemeat. And while everyone's eyes grew with anticipation, I heard the back door swing open, followed by a stomping of feet. Because we hadn't heard a vehicle, I knew it must be Jack, and I saw from Rita's expression that she assumed the same.

Sure enough, we heard the forced heartiness of his usual greeting. "Anybody awake here?"

"Merry Christmas, Jack!" Stan bellowed. "Just in time for dessert."

Jack entered with a package in each hand—one a bottle of some kind, and the other a small box. He handed the bottle-shaped present to Stan. He handed the box to Rita, who didn't even look at it, but fixed a cold stare on him.

"Oh boy, do those pies look good!" Jack grabbed a chair, pulling up between Oscar and Muriel.

Stan peeled the wrapping off his present, which was a very expensive brand of whiskey, and after studying the bottle, he looked at Jack with much the same indignant expression as Rita's.

"Merry Christmas, Stan!" Jack shouted.

"Well, thank you," Stan said.

I gazed at the small rectangular box Jack had given my wife, and at the expression still frozen on her face, and a bitter anger burned a hole in my stomach.

I stood. "Jack, I got something I need to show you."

He looked at me sideways, not fooled for a minute. "Oh?"

"Yeah, it'll just take a second." I motioned with my head toward the hallway. Jack looked down, shaking his head, but he rose slowly and followed. I ducked into the closest bedroom, and when Jack sauntered in and settled onto the bed, I swung the door shut.

"What the hell do you think you're doing?" I asked.

He held out both hands, palms up. "Not sure what you mean, Blake."

"Don't give me that. What are you thinking, giving a present to Rita?"

"I can't give my sister-in-law a Christmas present?"

I bit my lip, and took a step closer to him. "Jack, you know damn well how uncomfortable Rita is about even having you here. You need to start showing some consideration."

"And why is that?"

I sighed. "Listen, Jack…Bob hired you, so yeah…you've got every right to be here, but we've got our own little family here now. Things have changed."

"You can say that again."

"I'm simply asking you to show some respect for my family."

Jack looked at me with a fire that was more than angry. It was a hatred like I'd never seen from any man. And when he spoke, his voice sounded like no voice I'd ever heard before, either, so choked off by feeling that he couldn't contain it. As if something was about to burst from his throat.

"That was my family," he spit. "That's *my* wife."

"That *was* your wife," I said through my teeth.

"You stole my family."

"No, Jack. You lost them. You gave up on them, and you lost them."

"You had your eye on that woman from the day she stepped off the train."

I could not deny this, but of course this was beside the point. I held my tongue.

"You couldn't wait for the day you could step in."

"Jack, what I wanted doesn't matter one damn bit. You disappeared. Did you ever think about how that affected Rita? You were her husband, for christ's sake, and you didn't even bother to tell her you were alive."

"That was our business. That was my family, and that was our business."

"Well, this might be hard to believe, but the choices you made affected a lot more people than just you and Rita."

Jack suddenly looked baffled, as if this possibility had never once occurred to him. But he quickly recovered. With his defiance restored, he stood up.

"Who put you in charge here anyway? Since when are you the boss? I'm your older brother, goddamit." And he shoved me.

I was tempted to hit him. I've never wanted to hit anyone so bad. Instead, I balled my fists and held them up to his face. I showed them to him, and I said, "You left, Jack. You had a chance to have everything, and you blew it."

Jack glared at me, telling me with his expression that nothing I said even registered. He only saw obstacles.

Everything and everybody was an obstacle. He said nothing more, and finally left the room.

I heard his footsteps stomping toward the back door, and a slam followed.

When I joined the family moments later, I could practically see blood leaking from the corners of their mouths from biting their tongues.

I was just about to say something when the back door swung open again and Jack stormed in, and every horrible thought I could possibly imagine rushed into my head. I tried to remember where the nearest gun was, or what I could do to protect my family, before I noticed Teddy striding behind his father.

Jack stopped as he entered the dining room, and Teddy shouldered past him. Both of their faces were drained of color. Teddy's eyes were moist, his mouth pinched.

"Teddy, what is it?" Rita stood.

Teddy started crying, his face folding into an expression of pure sorrow.

"Is it Jenny?"

He nodded, and Rita wrapped her arms around him. Teddy's face fell into her, bouncing off her shoulder.

"Dammit," I muttered. "God dammit."

Oscar stood, almost unnoticed by the rest of us. But when his fist hit the wall, breaking clean through, it shook the whole house.

Chapter 19

We lost many people to the Depression. It just took some longer to die.

Jenny Glasser escaped the watchful eye of her daughter and husband for just a few minutes, snuck off to the barn, and draped a rawhide rope over a crossbeam. The milk stool she stepped off was so short that her toes were touching the ground when Steve found her.

I never comprehended the word 'inconsolable' until I watched Steve at his wife's funeral. Each time it seemed as if he'd regained his composure, he broke down again. And each time, he fell against Margie, whose own grief was supported by the solid shoulder of my nephew Teddy. I saw the same determination in Teddy's face that I'd had as a young man—the determination to not be mastered by this overpowering sorrow.

Pastor Ludke also had to be propped up, but not because of his emotions. He'd broken his hip early that fall, so Oscar stood at his side, a hand tucked in the old preacher's elbow. The good pastor had scheduled the service for early afternoon to take advantage of the warmest part of the day. But as he delivered a short eulogy, we sat with our shoulders slumped, our breath rising in wispy clouds. The woodstove in the corner of the Little Missouri Lutheran Church did little to fight the deep, crisp cold. The thermometer read well below freezing that morning, and still lingered near that mark.

Steve declined our offer to arrange a gathering afterward, so we all went home, which felt a little strange but also right somehow. Steve and Margie didn't even want to come over for something to eat. But Rita insisted that we take some hot dishes over to their house. After she and

Muriel prepared supper, I loaded boxes of chicken and potatoes into the car. When Steve answered, his eyes were still red.

Teddy came out from the dining room. "Hey, Blake."

"Thank you, Blake," Steve said. "Turns out you're the seventh person to come by with food. We have enough to feed us for a year."

I nodded, and handed the boxes over. "Well, just add those to the pile then, I guess."

"We sure do appreciate it."

We talked for a minute, but it quickly became awkward.

"Well I won't keep you, but if there's anything else at all, you let us know."

Steve set the boxes down, and we shook hands.

Back at the house, we gathered for supper.

"How's Steve?" Rita asked.

"Seems to be doin' okay. They've had a bunch of visitors."

Stan nodded. "Good."

"That is good," Rita agreed.

We ate slowly. We spoke little. We didn't make eye contact. Even Stan was silent. Only Oscar seemed anxious to eat, shoveling his food, the fist-sized puncture in the wall just above his head. When he'd cleaned his plate, he stood, stretched, picking up his plate and silverware.

"Excuse me, everyone."

"Certainly, Oscar," Rita said.

"You goin' to bed?" I asked.

"Thinking about it. Why? You need me to do something?"

"Well, I thought we might play some cards, and we could probably use another player."

Oscar hesitated, looking down at his plate. "I might sit in for a few hands."

"Good."

After taking his dishes into the kitchen, Oscar retired to the living room where he sat in his usual corner chair, out of sight. He turned on the radio, and cigarette smoke drifted from the corner.

Once we finished eating, I tried to drum up some interest in cards. Nobody protested, but there wasn't much enthusiasm. Stan and Muriel went to their room and had a long discussion. I did the dishes while Rita fed Benjamin. I hoped Oscar didn't lose interest before everyone came back.

"Nice service." Rita came into the kitchen after putting Benjamin to bed.

"Very nice."

Rita picked up a dishtowel and started drying. "You're quiet."

"Am I?"

"You've hardly said a word all afternoon."

"It's a sad day."

"Yes it is," she agreed.

Stan and Muriel emerged from the bedroom, and Muriel sidled up to us. "I don't think we're much in the mood for cards, Blake."

"Oh come on."

"Sorry," Muriel said.

"What are you going to do instead?"

"I don't know," Stan answered. "We might just go to bed."

"Just a few hands?" I asked.

Stan and Muriel exchanged a look. "I don't think so, Blake. We're pretty whipped."

"What's going on around here?"

There was a brief silence, during which Rita, Muriel, and Stan all looked at me with puzzled expressions.

"Blake, what are you talking about?" Stan said. "We just don't feel like playing, that's all."

"But I asked Oscar to stay up."

"Honey." Rita put a hand on my forearm. "It's been a long day. Maybe we should forget about cards for today."

"You don't want to play either?" I pointed toward the living room. "What about him?"

"Blake, what's gotten into you?" Rita asked.

"We need to play cards." The statement exploded from within me.

For reasons I couldn't begin to understand, each time someone turned away from my suggestion, it felt it like a bruise inside. It was ridiculous, I knew. I poured a cup of coffee and went to the living room, where I sat down in the chair next to Oscar. Stan and Muriel said goodnight. Benjamin started fussing, so Rita disappeared into our room with him.

"Doesn't look like anybody wants to play," I said to Oscar. "Sorry to keep you up."

He raised his brow, and his spectacles fell down his nose. "Well, that's all right. I could use some sleep myself. It's been a rough couple of days." He stood. "I'll see you in the morning."

"Night."

And so it was me.

I'm a man who spends a good portion of his time alone. Well over fifty percent. I love being alone. I love driving around the ranch to check on the cattle, or study the grass. I love walking through a field of alfalfa and breathing that sweet, rich aroma. I love the grip of long grass around my ankles when I wade through a meadow. I love being in a pasture, on a horse, weaving through a herd of cattle and their curious, cud-chewing wonder. The satisfaction I get from my life in this barren corner of Montana is as complete as I can imagine. My life would still be worthwhile and meaningful to me without any payoff. The Depression proved that.

But for some reason, that feeling disappeared that night after Jenny Glasser's funeral. Rita had a hard time getting Benjamin to sleep, and I knew that if I went in there, it would complicate matters. So I sat alone in the living room, wishing for company, and wondering how Jenny Glasser, a woman so blessed with a wonderful husband, and daughter, and a life so full and abundant, could possibly think about putting such a brutal end to all this goodness.

Chapter 20

My heels dragged along the dusty ground, leaving scuffs behind, as Oscar and I approached the house. The western sky glowed orange, and the black of night hovered, threatening to elbow its way in.

"I don't think I've ever been so tired in my whole life," I told Oscar.

"You need a vacation."

I scoffed. Suddenly Rita burst from the house. She grabbed my elbow and pulled me to the side. Oscar stopped and looked at us with uncertainty before recognizing that Rita needed to see me alone.

I wanted more than anything to go inside and sit. "What's going on?" I asked.

"Blake, when I was in town today, I went to the dry goods store. I've been reading that book, you know...the one about poisons…and I made a list of some things." She pulled me nearer, holding her mouth very close to my ear. "Blake, I asked Estelle whether anyone from our ranch had bought any of the things on that list."

I only had to look at her to know the answer to that question. Her eyes were as big as headlights.

"Who was it?" I asked.

"Well, at first they said they didn't have a record of anyone from our family buying any of the things on the list. And I was just about to leave when I thought to ask them one more thing." She looked at me and raised her brow.

"David Westford?" I asked.

Rita nodded with the gravity of a minister at a funeral.

I felt like crying and my knees rubbered on me. "God dammit."

Rita wrapped an arm around my waist. Still, I had to sit. I sank onto the stoop, realizing how much I did not want to believe this. And I thought about all the years I'd wondered about the death of my brother George. And how hard I'd worked to convince myself that it must have been an accident, that spilling blood did not count among the crimes my older brother might consider. "What are we gonna do? How are we going to live with them?"

"We need to report this," Rita said.

I held my head with both hands. "Do you think they'd have to dig up his body?"

Rita laid her head on my shoulder. "I don't know. God, I hope not."

"We need to report this to somebody besides Buddy. It won't go anywhere if we tell him."

Rita nodded. "I agree."

I let my head drop to my knees. "God, I hate this."

"There's something else, Blake. Something I can't figure out."

I turned to her, the bruise on my heart already much too tender.

"When I was at the bank, I decided to check on the ranch account since you didn't get a chance to do that last time."

I sighed. "Oh no."

"That's the strange part, Blake. The balance is higher."

My head jerked back like a string had tugged it from behind. "Higher?"

"Much, much higher."

"How much?"

"Thousands of dollars."

"Good lord."

"So I asked to look at the transactions, and it was Jack."

I sighed, shaking my head.

The very next night I followed through on something that Rita and I had discussed. I rang up the short-long-long phone number to Bob and Helen's house. Bob answered.

"Bob, we need to have a meeting."

"A meeting?"

"Yes…we need to discuss some business."

"Oh really?"

The silence that followed was filled with a feeling I couldn't identify. Something strong and frightening, almost like an odor.

"Who do you want at this meeting?"

"Well, you, of course, and Jack…and your wife."

A muffled mumbling followed. He came back on line. "All right."

We figured out a time that worked for everyone. I hung up, and Rita appeared next to me.

"Thursday night."

Rita nodded, but her eyes clouded with an unfamiliar fear.

Rita set cups and saucers on the table, along with a plate of cookies. I lit a cigarette and realized I already had one going, and that my chest already hurt from the countless others I'd smoked that evening. A knock sounded, and I jumped to my feet.

As Helen, Bob, and Jack entered the house, we exchanged cheerful greetings, greetings so forced that we all grinned at the absurdity. We sat at the table, poured coffee, chewed on the edges of cookies, and smoked and cleared our throats. I found myself studying the cups, watching them all the time to make sure Helen wasn't anywhere near anyone else's cup.

"Well…" I finally said, with the energy of breaking through a starting gate. "What's going on with this money?"

Helen's eyes got wide. "What money?" She spoke with a playful air, and it gave me a very bad feeling. I saw the same thing in Rita's face.

I turned directly to Jack. "Jack?"

Jack scooted forward in his chair. "Blake, we're taking over the ranch."

Rita and I said in unison, "What did you say?"

"Bob and I are going to take over the ranch."

I shook my head, as if trying to wake myself up. "What do you mean, take over? There's nobody to take it over from…we're all here…we're all working here together."

Jack sighed, turning a sly grin toward Bob, who looked down at his feet. "Well, that's just the thing, Blake. We actually want you to leave. We think it's time for a change."

"You people have got to be out of your everlovin' minds," Rita said.

Jack tilted his head and a grin came to his face that made me want to stand up and punch the life right out of him. "Well, as a matter of fact, we're not, Rita. We've talked to some legal people, and since we make up the majority of the owners of the ranch, we can ask you to leave if we decide to do that."

"Just like that," Rita said.

I started chuckling.

"What's so funny?" Rita turned to me with a look that could kill the strongest bull.

"Oh, nothing."

Jack leaned forward, resting his weight on his elbow. "Seriously, Blake…what's so funny?'

I just shook my head.

"Blake, we're not kidding," Jack said.

"Oh, I know…that's what's so funny." I stood up. "I think you guys better get out."

Jack, Helen, and Bob exchanged confused looks. "But Blake, we're not done talking. We need to discuss this some more," Helen said.

"No, I don't think you quite understand," I said. "I said I think you better leave. Because if you don't...Jack…." I turned toward my older brother. "If you don't leave, I'm going to pound your head right through this table." I slapped my hand against the table with a force that made everyone jump. A shout escaped Bob's throat.

As frightened as everyone looked at that moment, it didn't compare to my own fear, of my own anger. I felt as if I could kill these people. I wanted to. And the nervous energy that this feeling generated brought all three of them to their feet without a word of consultation. They barely had to look at each other to know that none of them felt safe. Jack said a very brief goodbye, but neither Bob nor Helen said a word. My wife took one look at me and said, "Blake, what on earth is going on?"

Chapter 21

The following Thursday, Oscar and I plowed through the first snowfall of winter toward Belle Fourche. A few cars had preceded us so we had ruts to follow, and could see where we needed to swerve to avoid getting stuck. The thick, soft blanket muffled the world, and the sun bounced a blinding reflection off the pure white.

The previous week had been tense, with tempers short and jaws clenched. We had gone out of our way to avoid those from the other house, but it was hard work. I was relieved to be getting away.

Oscar was talkative, recounting the most recent developments with Georgia. This was also a welcome relief from my own muddled thoughts.

"Blake, I tell you, this girl kisses like she needs it to stay alive." He clenched his massive fist. "She sucks the life right out of me."

"Hm." After a year and a half, Oscar's frank delivery of just about everything still made me uncomfortable. But it had never deterred him, if he even noticed.

"And I'm sure you know, Blake, that when a girl kisses you like that, it's damn hard to keep your hands where they belong, you know?"

"I imagine so."

Oscar squirmed in his seat, and his hands drifted out in front of him as if they explored the object of his affection as he spoke. "Oh, you bet your life it is, Blake. It's like having a piece of warm chocolate rubbed across your lips, and being told you can't take a bite."

I chuckled, mostly out of discomfort.

"I'm not kidding, Blake. It's a special kind of torture."

"So does Georgia know you're coming to town?"

He shook his head. "I couldn't get a hold of her."

"It'll be fun to surprise her, then."

Oscar nodded, a slow smile curling his mouth. He pushed his glasses up his nose.

I started to mention that I'd dated a woman in Belle Fourche myself a few years ago, but when I thought about how that story ended, with Sophie's surprise engagement to a local banker, I decided to keep that story to myself.

Once we arrived in Belle, we picked up three hundred pounds of soy cake and two hundred pounds of corn, then made our way to the market. The streets bustled, as they always did on sale day. Walking into the market, I unsnapped my shirt pocket and plucked Rita's grocery list from inside. Then I stopped dead for a moment, and even reached to hold Oscar back. But he had already whisked past me. A young guy leaned elbow-first on Georgia's counter, his hat tipped way back on his head, a big ol' grin stretching his face. Oscar paused, but a second look revealed that Georgia had her back to this guy, rearranging items on the shelves behind her counter. Oscar started toward her again.

I called to him, but either he didn't hear me or he ignored me. His shoulders rolled with purpose as he marched toward them. Georgia looked up and when she saw Oscar, a big smile formed.

"Oscar! What a nice surprise!"

Oscar's shoulders relaxed as he sidled up to the counter, just a few feet away from the cowboy. The young guy stretched himself out, standing a head taller than Oscar. He hooked his thumbs in his belt loops. He was slender, wearing a sheepskin coat and a tight blue western shirt with a black yolk. His dungarees showed an unusual amount of preparation, with a thin pleat running the length in front. His black cowboy boots were buffed to a bright shine. His hair was also black, under a black felt hat.

"How ya doin', Georgia?" Oscar asked.

"I'm great now." Her cheeks flushed. "I'm so happy to see you."

A sour look came over the young cowboy's face, but Georgia and Oscar's immersion excluded all else.

"You busy after work?" Oscar asked.

"She sure is," the other guy said.

"No I'm not," Georgia said, still looking at Oscar, who dug his fists deep into his pockets, smiling with a devilish look.

"You said you were busy," the cowboy said.

"Guess she was trying to give you a little message there, fella," Oscar said pleasantly.

Without any warning, the young guy's arm whipped forward, the knot of a fist taking a direct line toward Oscar's head. But as unexpected as the punch seemed, and as unprepared as Oscar appeared, his hand popped out of his pocket and caught the kid's chin with an almost effortless pump. The kid's teeth cracked and Georgia jumped, letting out a small whoop. Oscar didn't hit him hard, not nearly as hard as he could hit a man. But the kid staggered backward ten feet, his hand clamping his jaw. Blood trickled from one corner of his mouth. He repeated "Oh, oh oh" in about twenty staccato bursts, while Oscar stood looking at him, a slight grin on his face.

"Oscar," Georgia scolded, but her smile had grown even wider.

"Poor bastard," Oscar muttered.

The young guy stumbled out of the store, saying not a word. Oscar looked at me.

"Nice job," I said. "Very efficient."

"You're so cruel," Georgia said.

"That's right," Oscar agreed, adopting a ferocious frown. He looked comical glaring through his spectacles. Georgia kissed him on the cheek.

I began wandering the aisles, gathering my supplies, while the lovebirds whispered.

"Hey Blake!" Oscar called.

"Yes, Mr. MacArthur." I emerged from the rows of shelves.

"How late are we gonna be in town?"

"With this snow, I don't want to drive home too late," I said. "How late you working, Georgia?"

"I'm stuck here 'til six, Mr. Arbuckle."

"Why don't you stay the night, Oscar? You know some folks that have an extra bunk, right? And I'm sure we can find somebody from up our way that's spending the night. Or you can catch the mail truck in the morning."

"What about feeding?"

"I can handle it. Or I'll give Teddy a call if I need him."

"Oscar, don't put them out like that," Georgia said, but her expression was undeniably hopeful.

"Bull," I said. "Have a good time. You guys haven't seen each other much lately."

"Thank you, Mr. Arbuckle," Georgia said.

"Yeah…thanks a lot, Blake." Oscar's face turned pink.

Following our afternoon at the auction yards, I dropped Oscar at the market and wished him luck. I was actually relieved to be alone for a while. I had a couple of stops I hoped to make on my own. So after I dropped Oscar off, I stopped by a non-descript downtown building. A nervous woman in a beige suit that looked like a military uniform greeted me.

"If it's possible, I'd like to talk with Mr. Barbury," I announced. "I don't have an appointment, but I did tell him I might be stopping by."

"Your name, please?" The woman ran a finger down an appointment book.

"Blake Arbuckle."

"I don't see your name here, Mr. Arbuckle."

"Yes, ma'am. I don't have an appointment. Could you please ask Mr. Barbury if he has a few minutes? If he doesn't, I'll come back another time."

She looked up at me. "Mr. Barbury almost never sees someone without an appointment."

"Yes, I'm sure that's true." I smiled.

After a frown that formed an impressively tight curl, she bounced out of her chair into an office behind her. A moment later, she poked her head out and nodded. I entered as she eased past me on her way out.

Tony Barbury was an impressive figure, a man with bearing. Tall and big, with black hair and a mustache that looked like it was made of steel.

"What can I do for you, Mr. Arbuckle?"

For the next hour I laid out everything. All the facts, all my suspicions. All my questions. Barbury was kind and patient enough to listen to the whole thing without telling me I was out of my mind. He asked excellent questions and studied the items I'd brought. And by the time I left, I had hope that something good could happen.

Just after dark, I took off for the ranch. The snow had drifted in a lazy swirl all day, and I was glad it was sale day, as there had been more traffic than usual leaving town. The tracks were well drawn, but the snow had piled high so I had to drive slowly. For the first twenty miles a small group of cars traveled together, but the others turned off the main road one at a time. My solitary beams poked holes into the black night, catching tiny white flakes that sparked the sky. I had to keep my speed down to fifteen miles an hour on the good stretches, and even slower when the snow got deep.

The wind had died, but the cold nearly froze my fingers in a curl around the wheel. The heater whined, but it didn't seem to be providing much in the way of heat. My nose disappeared. My ears had gone numb. Moisture coated my upper lip, and I eventually had to stop wiping it when the skin became raw. I pounded my feet against the floor to keep the nerves alive.

As I rounded one curve the car plowed into a surprise drift and stopped. I ground the gears, forcing it into reverse, and gave it some gas. The car didn't move at first, and a slight panic settled into my gut. I revved the engine again and the car still didn't move. I shifted back into first and started a rocking motion, moving forward, then hitting the clutch so the car rolled back. Once I got some momentum, I jammed it into reverse, and the rear tires finally took hold. I backed up thirty feet, and rounded the drift. The car bucked with the bumpy terrain.

After rounding the drift, I got back to the road and continued my grim push forward. The snow started falling heavier. The windshield wipers began to gather ice until they smeared snow across my vision. I had to lean forward and peek through the bottom of the windshield to see. The snow began to cover the tracks in the road so I could barely see them even in those brief seconds when the window cleared. Fifteen minutes after my battle with the snow drift, the car came to another sudden stop.

I swore, putting a shoulder to the door. The door squawked as it broke through an icy shield. Cold air pinched my skin. Aside from the idling engine, the night was completely still. I studied my predicament, wishing I had Oscar with me. The car had come to rest against a small hump just off the side of the road. A large clump of sagebrush lodged into the right front wheel well. I crouched next to the right bumper, locked my hands underneath, and leaned into the car while lifting. The car didn't budge and when I tried putting more effort into the next push, my boot slipped and my knee hit the icy ground.

I swore, stood and limped back to the driver's seat. I climbed inside and tried backing up slowly, easing out the clutch. The car didn't move. So I wound the engine tighter and popped the clutch. Still nothing. I tried going forward, but got nowhere.

I had no choice but to keep trying, but alternating between forward and reverse proved useless. I tried pushing again. My knee stiffened, and the cold settled deeper into my bones, freezing my joints. I felt like a piece of cold machinery, where even the grease had no effect. I tried wedging a bag of feed behind the rear tires, but the car had sunk too low into the icy snow. There was no room. So I broke open a bag of soy cake and spread a layer behind the rear tires, sniffing away the cold moisture running down my lip. My eyes watered. Every limb had gone numb. The car still did not move. At all.

Eventually I had to concede that the car wasn't going anywhere, and I had to think about surviving—about keeping warm without running out of gas.

I killed the engine and retrieved an old wool army blanket I kept in the trunk for this very purpose. I propped a couple of bags of corn on the passenger side, and wedged myself between them, wrapping myself in the blanket. I started to shiver. I tried to stop it. I tensed my muscles and moved my limbs. I slapped my face, my arms, my feet. But still my muscles quaked. So I turned the engine on and allowed myself the luxury of huddling up to the heater. Once the shivering stopped, I killed the engine again.

I repeated this several times, and also tried backing out again. I spread more soy cake, trying not to think about the waste. When it didn't help, I felt guilty about losing the feed. I emptied the gas can we kept in the trunk, wondering how much gas I had left, how much longer I could run the engine. As the night swallowed me and the numb feeling moved further up my limbs, closer to my torso, I began to worry.

Every time I heard stories about people freezing to death after they wandered away from their cars or their homes, I wondered what they must have been thinking. It was such common knowledge that you need to stay where you are. But the longer I sat in one place, the deeper that cold sank into my bones, until it felt as if the bones themselves had turned to ice. The hope of ever feeling warm again started to slip away, and thoughts of running began to sound logical. Thoughts of a farmhouse within walking distance.

I had to fight the pull of these thoughts. First in my head, and then out loud. I told myself in words not to get out of the car. I held myself in the car seat and talked to myself like a child, scolding myself for such ridiculous ideas. It worked, and then it didn't. I thought back to Stan's situation, amazed that he hadn't given in to this temptation. I argued with myself for a very long time, and it was exhausting. But it also kept my mind occupied. It kept me awake. It might have even kept me just a little bit warmer. I piled more bags of feed into the front seat. I did whatever I could to keep busy. I buried myself in the bags of feed. I ran the heater.

Three hours after it started, a brief flicker shone in my rearview mirror and I turned to see headlights peering through the night. I started laughing and crying at the same time as I scrambled to free myself from the feed bags. I flung open the driver's door and threw my body onto the road, falling to my hands and knees. I scrambled to my feet and waved my arms, shouting and laughing like a lunatic.

When the car stopped, and the blinding lights were past me, and I could see the car clearly, I realized it was Bob.

"Oh my god." I hobbled to the driver's door, and the window lowered. Jack was behind the wheel, and Bob slept on the passenger side, his head propped against the window. The warm air spilling from the car smelled like a gin mill.

"You need some help there, stranger?" Jack said, fixing bleary eyes on me.

"You guys got a rope?" My chest felt completely filled with air.

"Bob." Jack gave Bob's shoulder a shove.

Bob blinked, without moving. "What's the matter? What's wrong?"

"Look who needs a rope."

"A rope? What the hell? Are we stuck?"

"No, we're not stuck, you damn fool. Blake here is."

"Oh... Hey Blake." Bob leaned forward, sitting dazed for a moment, staring straight ahead.

Jack turned to me, and I didn't like the smile on his face. "What do you think we oughta do, Bob?"

Bob rotated his head sideways, and I realized he was much drunker than Jack. "What?" was all he could manage.

Jack kept smiling up at me. "So brother Blake needs our help."

"Come on, Jack. Is there a rope in the trunk?"

"Well..." Jack stared out the front windshield. "Hell, I'm not really sure, Blake. This is Bob's car." He turned to Bob. "Bob, you got a rope in here?"

Bob's head rolled toward us, then back in the other direction again. "I think so."

Jack smiled up at me. "He thinks so." Jack made no move to open the trunk, or give me the key. He turned back toward the steering wheel and started nodding slowly. "Looks like we probably do got a rope then." I shivered, only partly from the cold.

"You going to get it?" I finally asked.

"Well…" Jack turned to me, and the smile was gone. "Maybe we might have to work out a deal here, Blake."

"A deal?"

"Yeah…a deal."

I bent down, leaning on the car. "You're really going to ask me to bargain with you to save my goddam life?"

Jack looked behind him. "You think somebody else is gonna come along?" He looked at his watch. "Oh my…looks like it's gettin' awful late, Blake."

"Jack, give me the keys."

Jack turned to me with a bit of a fire in his eyes. "Now you're telling me?" He turned to Bob. "You hear that, Bob? Blake's telling me to give him the keys. You think I oughta do what he tells me?"

"Yeah, do what he tells ya," Bob mumbled. "He's the boss."

Jack laughed. "That's rich. I like that." He pounded Bob on the back. "You're a funny man, Bob."

My joints were freezing into place. The cold had burrowed deep, through my clothes, under the skin, and straight to the bone.

"Jack, come on. This isn't funny," I said. "I'm freezin' out here."

"Maybe you should get in your car," Jack said.

I glared at him, then thought better of it, looking out across the muted white landscape around us. Jack sighed once.

"You know what your problem is, Blake?"

"No, Jack, but I've been dying for someone to tell me."

Jack's smile disappeared. He scrutinized me, as if trying to decide whether I was worthy of his wisdom.

"You have no idea what it's like to lose," Jack said.

"Oh really?"

He nodded. "That's right, Blake. You've had your life laid out for you…"

"Jack, everyone who lives out here knows more than a person ever needs to know about loss."

He just shook his head. "Nope."

"We lost the same things you did, Jack. We just stuck around anyway. That's the only damn difference."

Jack continued shaking his head, and I could see this conversation going nowhere. My feet were so numb that I felt like a miracle I was still standing. "What do you want, Jack? What kind of deal?"

"Oooooh. He's gettin' desperate." He smiled at me. "You're serious?"

"Just tell me, Jack. What do you want?"

Jack sniffled. He fixed a look on me, and the smile faded. Suddenly he didn't look one bit drunk. His face became like wood. Like a carving of a real man. "I want you to leave, Blake."

I stared hard at my brother, and the frigid air tucked my skin further and further inside itself. "You know that's not going to happen, Jack." And before the sentence had even reached its period, the engine revved, and Bob's car started moving.

The panic that dove straight to the middle of my heart just about stopped it. The snow prevented the car from accelerating very much, so I ran after it. His window was still down.

"Wait!" The shout hurt my chest.

The car slowed, and when I pulled up next to it, my lungs aching from gulping frozen air, I came face to face with that awful, sad smile.

When I got home, Rita stumbled out of the bedroom, eyes puffed with sleep, hair everywhere. She'd never looked so lovely. I wrapped her up, and her head fell against me with a tired tap.

"Oh honey. I was so worried."

"What time is it?"

"Almost three o'clock."

"I'm sorry. Everything's fine now."

"Are you sure? You're freezing, Blake." She put her palms on my face.

"I'm fine, sweetheart. The storm slowed me up, but the world's right again. How's that baby?"

"He's mad at you."

"Oh is he?"

"Yeah, he's been yelling at you all night."

"Well, I guess I better apologize in the morning." I tucked a strand of unruly hair behind Rita's ear.

"You better, or he might ignore you."

"What about you? Will you ignore me?"

"Maybe for a little while." Her hand settled behind my neck, softly tickling my hair.

"How long?" I kissed her forehead.

"At least fifteen minutes…maybe even longer if you're not real nice to me." Rita dug her fingers into my hair and ran her fingernails along my scalp. It felt better than anything I had ever felt in my life. I kissed her.

"It's really, really late, Blake," she said from the side of her mouth.

"Mm hm."

"So you better treat me like a woman right this minute if you expect to get any sleep." She wrapped her hand around my neck and pulled her head closer.

"I don't really feel like playin'." I slid a hand up the back of her nightgown.

"Oh my god, your hand is like a shovel." She pulled it away.

"Sorry. Maybe we oughta get under the covers. Warm up a little."

"I think that's an excellent plan."

We walked, arms around each other, to the bedroom. As I took off my clothes, my skin was so sensitive that it hurt. I pulled on my pajamas and it felt as if I was rubbing myself with dirt. But I kept this to myself as I crawled under the covers. Rita wore her nightgown to protect herself from my ice cold skin. But she wrapped her limbs around me and rubbed me all over. I began to warm up as I put my mouth to hers. We kissed like we hadn't for months, since before Benjamin was conceived, and it didn't take long for me to find my way inside her.

"You feel so good," I muttered.

"Do I?"

"Yes you do." I moved slow, and she danced along with me to a song we knew well.

"And why is that?"

"Because I missed you all day long."

"Did you really?"

"I surely did."

"Oh darlin'...you know how much I hate hearing that." She smiled up at me, and I kissed her nose and cheek.

"I know. It makes you feel real bad, doesn't it?" I started to speed up just a little.

"It makes me feel like...oh dear...oh dear..."

"Does that hurt?"

"Oh, it hurts real bad, you brute. Stop it right now." She smiled.

"Sorry, but I don't think I can do that."

"Oh? Why not?"

"Because I like it just a little too much." I sped up a little more.

"Just thinking of yourself, are you? What if I don't like it?"

"Well, it won't last much longer."

"Oh, you're so mean."

"I know. How do you put up with me?"

"Oh, I don't know. Oh god...please stop talking now."

Rita touched a finger to my lips and we settled into our song, singing the familiar harmonies and building to the final chorus, where the full orchestra joined in. What followed was a feeling of togetherness I did not imagine was possible, as if by entering Rita, I had punctured the deepest part of her, and she had spilled over me, replacing my icy skin with a layer of warmth and love and tenderness, and finally, gradually, soaking into me. The number of people in our house required a certain discretion in these circumstances, but this time, neither of us was able to control it. We both shouted, then covered each others' mouths. We collapsed into a final sigh, then began laughing quietly, whispering our love through the laughter.

Benjamin stirred and whimpered, but did not wake.

I fell asleep still inside Rita, and I have never slept like I did for the next three hours.

Chapter 22

I am not ashamed to admit that from that day forward, every time I heard the short-short-long ring that indicated a call coming in to Bob and Helen's house, I picked up the phone and listened. The disadvantages of a party line can also be advantages, after all. I'm sure they were doing the same. Between the party line and the mail coming in one bag, there were few secrets in our world. I had to instruct Tony Barbury to send information in blank envelopes, and I couldn't risk taking his phone calls. Even making them was risky. So I limited my calls to letting him know when I'd be in town. No information.

I did not tell Rita about my deal with Jack because I was convinced I'd be able to find a way around it. I even had two separate plans for accomplishing that. I was pretty sure the first one would work, but it had the potential of taking forever to come together. The second plan was one I was completely confident would work. But I didn't want to resort to that one until it was necessary. Jack gave me six months, until late August, to meet his demands. I didn't think anyone else knew about the deal. So for those six months, we engaged in a duel with pens and silent glares, packed with meaning. Those six months were the worst time of my life.

Winter stayed late that year, with heavy snow, which meant we could expect another good spring runoff. By March, when the snow had faded to a patchwork of alternating whites and tans, we were ready for the hard work ahead. The stock had wintered well, thanks to Oscar and Ole.

The ewes were about ready to lamb, and Bob and Jack and I decided it was time to invest in a lambing shed. Several neighbors had reported much higher survival rates among their newborns with a shed. The structure would be simple—long and narrow, with rows of small stalls on each side. As soon as the sun created enough of a clearing in the Big Meadow, we hauled the equipment out there and one warm spring day, Jack, Oscar, Bob and I began construction. The sun filtered through a very thin mist of clouds, dissolving the snow with a slow persistence and bringing moisture to our foreheads and down our backs, as if the snow evaporated directly from the ground into our clothes.

While Jack and Bob planted the posts to anchor the walls, Oscar and I followed behind, nailing planks to form the outside walls. We bought low-grade wood, which meant lots of splinters for Oscar, who refused to wear gloves. Every half hour I'd catch him digging at his palm or a thumb with a pocket knife.

"You gonna have any skin left by supper?"

He smiled, peering over his glasses.

"I brought an extra pair," I informed him.

"I know."

"Tell me again what it is you got against gloves?"

"My hands sweat, plus they're too damn clumsy."

"So you'd rather bleed?"

"Yep."

I shook my head.

There was little talk behind the rhythm of hammers and saws. The sun rose higher, and the smell of grass became stronger. The sweet smell made me a little sad. I loved this time of year, when the world wakes up. It smelled like morning. Like life. I didn't want to leave this.

"Jack, when are you gonna race that horse again?" Oscar asked.

Jack's brow raised for a moment, but he took a deep breath and smiled wryly. "Soon as you marry that girl of yours."

"You better not wait that long," I said. "He didn't even find out her name for three years."

"Mr. Arbuckle, I'll have you know that I have already proposed to Miss Georgia." Oscar pounded at a nail.

"You did?"

Oscar turned red.

"What'd she say?"

"What do you think?"

"You gonna bring her out here?"

Oscar pumped another nail into the plank. "She's not real thrilled with that idea."

"Did you tell her we'll feed her?"

"Yeah."

"And that we're the nicest folks you've ever met in your whole damn life?"

Oscar nodded. "She's a stubborn one, that girl."

"You two should get along just fine then."

"Ouch." Oscar studied his thumb, and I smiled to myself.

I watched Jack plunge a post hole-digger into the ground, his sinewy body lifting the double handles high, then burying the blades into the moist clay. I briefly pictured myself doing the same thing to his head.

That day, we put up the four walls of the sheep shed.

"Good work, guys," I said. "We got a hell of a lot done today."

"We sure did," Bob agreed.

"We should be able to get about half the stalls done tomorrow," I said.

"Oh..." Bob stopped. "I guess I forgot to mention that we won't be able to work on this tomorrow."

"What?"

"Yeah, we need to run to town tomorrow."

"You need to?" I actually started toward my brother, but Oscar reached out and blocked my path with his arm.

"Yeah, we need to get a few things done in town." Bob looked down at his boots.

"Well, you might have given us a little more notice," I said.

"It slipped my mind." Bob started toward his car.

"And Wednesday?" I couldn't hide my anger.

"We should be here."

"Should?" I stopped and faced my younger brother. "What's going on here, Bob? You need to show a little consideration. We have to make plans, too, you know."

"We'll be here Wednesday," Bob said.

I turned, shaking my head, muttering.

Bob and Jack crawled into Bob's car, and Oscar and I took off for home.

"What the hell is going on with those two?" Oscar asked.

"I wish I knew."

Oscar pushed his glasses up his nose, looking out the window.

We followed Bob's car back to the house, and I made no effort to offer the customary wave when we passed.

"Is that the sheriff?" Oscar asked.

I saw a car parked in front of our house. "Looks like it."

"What the hell is he doing here?" Oscar asked.

"That's a damn good question."

Buddy Walters sat at the dining room table, cradling a cup of coffee and rolling a cigarette. Rita sat across from him, bouncing Benjamin on her lap. Benjamin grabbed at her hair and Rita responded by kissing his neck, plucking her hair from his chubby fingers.

"Howdy, Blake." Buddy stood, reaching to shake.

"How you doin', Buddy?"

"All right. All right."

"Well don't stand on my account."

"Sure thing." He sat.

"You remember Oscar, of course." I gestured.

Buddy stood again. "How you doin', Oscar?"

"I'm going to go feed him." Rita stood, indicating Benjamin with a nod. She looked at me with questioning eyes, but with Buddy looking right at me, I could only try to convey with my eyes that I had no idea why Buddy was there.

As Rita disappeared into our bedroom, Oscar excused himself and started toward the stairs, but Buddy held out a hand.

"Mr. MacArthur, I'm sorry…but I actually need you to stay."

"Oh come on. What now?" I said.

Buddy danced in place. "Well, Mr. MacArthur…I've got something here I need you to take a look at." Buddy pulled a sheet of paper from his back pocket, and carefully unfolded it. He held it out to Oscar. "You know what this is?"

Oscar took the paper, and the minute he saw it, he groaned.

"What is it?" I asked.

Buddy cleared his throat. He fiddled with the handcuffs, pulling his keys from his pocket, fumbling to insert the tiny key into the tiny lock.

Oscar held the paper out to me. "It's the arrest record from back home."

I studied the document, which showed that Oscar MacArthur had been convicted of robbing a dry goods store. His sentence, as he had explained to me, was his exile to the West.

"Buddy, what the hell does this prove? This was fourteen years ago."

"Well, Blake…I'm not saying it proves anything, but I still need to take him in."

"No you don't."

Buddy looked at me like a kid who'd just been told he couldn't go on the Ferris wheel. "What're you talkin' about, Blake?"

"Show me something…anything…that says this gives you a reason to take him in. Give me a piece of evidence, for christ's sake."

Buddy looked at the floor, searching as if he'd lost his last nickel.

"Where'd you get this anyway?" I held up the paper.

"It was brought to my attention."

I chuckled. "That's what I thought." I resisted a strong temptation to make a comment about his abilities as a lawman. "Buddy, I think you should probably just head on back to Ekalaka and leave us be."

Buddy thought for a moment, and after a brief glance at each of us, I watched his mind making itself up behind those darting eyes. He left.

"Thank you, Blake. And I'm sorry," Oscar said.

"You got nothing to apologize for, my friend." I laid a hand on his shoulder. "You're stuck in the middle of something. You're the one who deserves an apology."

Chapter 23

Two days later, Jack and Bob joined us at the shed, as promised. They looked surprised to see Oscar, and I was seething, realizing that they knew about Buddy's visit. But we shouldered our work, with Jack and Bob punching the ground with post hole diggers, and Oscar prying splinters from his hands. The stalls came together in a slow progression of posts and planks. There was little talk on another perfect spring day in Montana. The birds appeared in a glorious formation, flying over as if they expected something exciting to happen. But after a while, even the stragglers lost interest, and flew off to explore other possibilities.

The pounding of hammers sang out, the sound bounding across the prairie, where echoes do not exist. At dinner time, we broke out some leftover fried chicken, with potato salad. Bob and Jack sat on the ground, leaning against the bottom plank of a stall. Oscar and I propped ourselves on the opposite side of the same stall, our legs stretched out, nearly touching theirs. Oscar dug at a splinter, and I pulled off my gloves, wiping my sweaty hands on my dungarees.

"We're gonna finish this side today," I said.

"Sure looks that way," Oscar agreed.

"So who's gonna be working the night shift when lambing starts?" Jack asked.

"You volunteering?" I asked.

"Hell no," Jack said. "I got enough going on with racing season coming."

"I was kidding, Jack. Ole said he'd stick around for lambing."

"Why not him?" Bob gestured toward Oscar with his chin.

Oscar looked up. "Him?"

Bob set his eyes on Oscar like bullets.

"You see me sitting here?" Oscar asked, pushing himself up a little straighter.

"Yeah, I see you."

"All right, hold on a second here," I said.

"Aw, just let 'em fight it out," Jack said.

"Shut up, Jack." I glared him into silence. "Bob, whatever it is that's going on between you and Oscar will not come out here into the fields…you understand? We got too much to do, and not enough…"

"He shoulda thought of that before…"

Oscar jumped to his feet and leaped across the stall in the time it took Bob to roll to his knees. And Oscar wrapped his meaty hands around Bob's throat before the rest of us moved. I embraced Oscar and tried to pull him off Bob, which was like trying to pry an iron band off a barrel.

"I never stole a dime and you know it," Oscar muttered through his teeth.

Bob coughed. "I guess I'm just supposed to take your word for that."

I bent down past Oscar, pushing my face close to Bob's. I whispered into his ear, "Dammit, Bob…you really think you're safe from those two? They're not going to stop until they get it all."

Bob made an effort to throw a punch, but Oscar's grip drained him of strength and his fist plunked against Oscar's shoulder with no effect.

"Look at what this has done to you," I said.

"How do you know it ain't true?" Jack had not moved from his side of the stall.

"That's a good one," I said.

"Well, that's just ignorant," Jack murmured.

"Coming from you, I'll take that as a compliment," I said.

Jack chuckled, shaking his head. "Damn, this family is messed up."

Despite my efforts, Oscar had not let up, and Bob's face had turned a frightening shade of blue. I tried digging a knuckle into Oscar's forearm to loosen his grip, but it was like pushing against oak. It actually hurt my knuckle.

"Oscar, you don't want to make this any worse than it already is. Come on, buddy. Let go of him," I whispered into his ear. "He's not the problem." I grabbed Oscar's hand, and with a firm but steady pressure, tried pulling it free. Finally, he began to ease up. Oscar's face also flushed, more red than purple. A bright, fiery red. At last, he let go and stood up, stepping back from Bob, who held his throat and coughed. Bob raised his head, and with his eyes closed, took several deep, purposeful breaths. When he got his air back, his jaw set into a stiff jut. He opened his eyes, but instead of turning his angry gaze at Oscar, he looked directly at me and pointed.

"You have no right."

I shrugged. "You can fool yourself for as long as you want, Bob. No skin off my nose.

Chapter 24

During our night shifts in the lambing shed, Ole Stenjham walked through the rows of sleeping and nursing ewes like a shadow, without sound, never tripping or kicking a dirt clod, or scuffing a heel. Ole could duck into a stall to check on a new lamb, clear its nostrils, help it find a teat, clean off the excess afterbirth, and do it in complete silence, even lifting the latch without a sound.

During the day, the shed resembled an untended schoolroom. The lambs cried, the mothers scolding or attempting to explain. With two thousand head, three of us needed to be present at a time, so Bob, Jack, Oscar, Ole, and I rotated shifts. I tried to make sure that Oscar and Bob didn't work together, but one day, Jack hadn't returned from a trip to town for a tractor part, and Ole had taken the night shift. So Bob, Oscar, and I tended the sheep.

Oscar looked for new lambs while Bob pitched hay into the pens. I nursed an injured ewe, trying to apply some iodine to the cut she'd gotten from a barbed wire fence. Oscar sauntered into the shed, cradling a tiny newborn in his arms.

"We lost a lamb this morning, right?" he asked.

"Yeah."

"Where's the mama?"

"Not sure…did we let her out?"

"She's down at the end," Bob called from the opposite side of the shed.

"Thanks." Oscar trudged toward the end of the long row of stalls, the lamb's ears flopping, his legs swinging as if they had tiny hinges.

"We lost a ewe?" I asked.

"Yeah. Mutt."

"Mutt? Damn." I stepped out from my stall and followed Oscar, knowing he'd need a hand. I dreaded telling Teddy about Mutt, a ewe that he'd nursed as an orphan. The little lamb had followed Teddy and his dog Pup around until she thought she was a dog, which had prompted George, Jr. to come up with her ingenious nickname, short for mutton.

"So where's the dead one?" Oscar asked. "Out back?"

"Yeah."

Oscar opened the door to the stall across from the lone ewe and set the newborn lamb in the straw. Then he went outside and returned, carrying the dead lamb.

"I'll go get some twine," I said.

Oscar nodded.

When I returned to the stall, I watched Oscar bury his buck knife into the dead lamb's gut, splitting its belly. He then skinned the wooly hide with a dexterity I admired. He split each leg up the inside, peeling the hide from the muscles, the blood spreading in a thin sheen across the silver blade. When the skin from the four legs hung like tongues from the corpse, he began separating the hide from the lamb's back, peeling it away as he carefully trimmed the fat and muscle that gripped the skin. When he finished, he had one big piece of lamb-shaped hide.

"All right," Oscar said. "Let's put some clothes on that baby."

We entered the stall where the newborn lay bleating, its look blank.

"We're gonna give you a new coat, little fella," Oscar announced.

He poked holes along the edges of the hide, and together we stood the lamb up. I held it steady while Oscar arranged the hide along its back. I kept the hide in place while Oscar unraveled the twine, threading it through one of the holes. For the next fifteen minutes Oscar weaved the twine back and forth under the lamb's belly and around its legs, securing the dead lamb's hide to the live one's body.

Oscar stood up. "What do you think?"

"He shouldn't have any problem at all gettin' a date."

"He's lookin' real handsome." Oscar pushed a knuckle against his glasses, and looked toward the other stall. "Let's see if that mama likes him as much as we do."

Oscar scooped up the baby and carried him across the shed, where I unlatched the gate for the stall where the ewe stood in one corner. She ducked her head, ready to escape if the opportunity presented itself. Oscar set the lamb on its tiny hooves near the ewe's bag. I closed the gate. The ewe moved, and Oscar picked up the lamb and repositioned him near her nose, so she could smell the hide. She pressed her moist nose against the lamb's flank, bobbing along his side.

Oscar stepped away, and we watched, knowing this was the crucial moment. The ewe looked away from the lamb for a moment, turning her gaze to us, as if questioning our judgement.

"Okay, so he's not yours, but he's a nice little fella," Oscar said.

"Give him a chance," I added.

"What are you guys up to?" Bob was suddenly behind us, and every being in the stall jumped. The lamb fell to its knees, and the ewe scurried to the other side of the stall, behind us.

"Quiet, Bob," I whispered. "Damn."

Oscar helped the lamb to its feet but the ewe had become jumpy. She buried her nose in the corner of the stall. Oscar carried the lamb near the ewe's head, moving deliberately. He set the lamb on its pins again, and backed away. The ewe hesitated but sniffed the hide. She touched her nose to the lamb's. The lamb bleated.

I took a chance and crept toward the lamb, lifting it and setting it next to the ewe's bag again. I cupped a palm under the lamb's chin and lifted it to the bag. I grabbed one of the swollen teats, squeezing a stream of milk onto the lamb's nose. I held the teat to its mouth. He bobbed his head a couple of times, then tasted the milk. His tongue slipped from his mouth and snaked around the teat. He pulled it inside his mouth and sucked.

The ewe did not move away. And for the next several minutes, they provided us with a fine little scene of domestic bliss. The lamb suckled, and the ewe turned her head from time to time, bleating her approval.

"Good work," I told Oscar.

He nodded once.

I turned to Bob. "What the hell were you thinking, scaring him like that?"

"Sorry about that. Didn't realize what you guys were doing." Bob removed his hat and rubbed the top of his head with the hand that held it.

Bob's manner made me nervous. It had been a long time since he'd been civil to either of us.

"No harm done," I said. "It looks like he's gonna be fine now."

"Listen…" Bob looked at his boots and put his hat on, covering his face. "While things are a little bit quiet here…I was wondering if I could talk to you." Bob's voice started shaking like a tin roof in a windstorm.

"Sure, Bob." I opened the gate to the stall and we settled onto the top plank, locking our heels in the plank below. Oscar stood off to the side, and finally asked, "You want me to make myself scarce for a bit?"

"If you don't mind," Bob muttered.

"Not at all." Oscar went outside

I studied Bob, whose complexion had faded as white as new wool. "What's on your mind?"

"Well…"

I thought Bob might fall right off the plank, his limbs shook so much.

"The thing is, Blake…well, I been thinking…" Bob's throat seemed to block up, and he held a hand to his chest. He coughed a couple of times. "Well..." Bob met my eye but only briefly. His round face clenched like fingers around a gun. And then I watched my brother go through an internal battle with himself that just about tore me apart. I can't imagine what it must have felt like. His chin dropped to his chest, and his eyes closed, and he grimaced as if he was in the worst kind of physical pain, as if every organ inside him was at war. Part of me wanted to tell him to just forget about it…that whatever he wanted to tell me wasn't worth this kind of pain. But I held my tongue, and allowed the battle to play itself out.

But he lost. Or the better part of him did, anyway. He couldn't do it. He shook his head, eyes still locked as tight as a storm cellar.

"I'm sorry, Blake." He climbed down off the plank, moving like a man who's just received a death sentence.

I wanted to say something…I wanted to somehow coax this secret from him. But I knew better than to even try.

Chapter 25

By this time I had given a lot of thought to the things that happened to our family during the Depression. All the loss of life…both human and beast, the betrayals, Jack's countless disappearances. I'm a man who likes to give people the benefit of the doubt, and when it came to my family members, during that period, I believed that most of it was driven by a desperate need to survive. I'd seen desperation lead to far more brutal crimes than stealing, or running away for a few years. Based on this, I'd forgiven a lot. And I had clung to the hope, despite so much evidence to the contrary, that Helen and Jack were basically good people whose judgment had been clouded by this need to survive.

But now, well…I didn't understand. The ranch was doing well enough to support everyone in the family. There was no need to compete. Except for one basic human need, of course. The seductive leer of greed. It saddened me to think that these people that I'd tried so hard to understand might be so selfish and greedy that they didn't care about the history of our family, or about working together to make things beneficial to everyone. They simply wanted everything. I couldn't comprehend this kind of ambition.

At the same time, I was fighting for my life, and part of me was willing to do whatever it took. So maybe I comprehended it better than I wanted to admit.

One day, a letter arrived with no return address, and my heart sped up. I checked the signature. As I'd hoped, the letter was from Tony Barbury. But once I skimmed the typed message, I closed my eyes. The information I had given him about the poison didn't provide enough reason to pursue a murder charge. It turned out the product was commonly used by horse people, to clean their saddles. He had researched the possibility of tracing the 'agent' in my father's body. He had learned that the technology for identifying this substance was very unreliable. From what he could determine, he didn't recommend putting the family through the inevitable trauma.

My chin dropped, and I held the bridge of my nose, pressing hard into my eyelids. I felt a trickle of moisture travel the length of my face.

"What's wrong?"

I felt a warm hand on my neck, the fingers rubbing lightly. Rita plucked the letter from my hand.

"Oh." I heard the disappointment in her voice. "Well, this last part sounds promising."

"What last part?" I wiped a forearm across my eyes.

Rita held the letter in front of me, pointing. I had overlooked a second paragraph. It said:

However, I think I do have some good news. I have been in contact with the Army Investigative Services, and they have informed me that Jack is still wanted for the charges of embezzlement. They will be contacting you soon to discuss this issue with you.

"Oh, thank God," I muttered.

We sat in silence for a moment, and for the first time in weeks, I felt as if I could breathe without a balloon in my chest.

"Blake?"

"Yeah?" I looked at Rita. Like me, she had a few new wrinkles around the eyes. Glints of silver peeked out from her thick dark hair.

"What's going on with you?"

"What do you mean?"

"Talking to you has been like yelling into a windstorm lately. You don't hear a word I say."

"Really?"

Rita nodded, and I placed a palm to her cheek, wishing I could brush away the concern on her face.

"This stuff is hard," I said.

"Well, it's hard for me, too," Rita said. "We shouldn't be taking it on separately...not without talking."

"You're right. I have been."

So we talked, but even then, my mind was clouded by the big secret I kept from Rita. The secret sat in the middle of that room like a crying baby that only I could hear. The secret demanded my attention, and when something is that needy, you can't ignore it. All else becomes secondary. My poor wife had no way of knowing that she was competing for my ear with such a powerful foe. I nodded in all the right places, said yes to all the right questions, and threw out a few thoughts of my own. But they were barely formed. They were almost not even real. But I guess they were convincing enough. Rita hugged me when we finished talking, and I didn't realize the conversation had ended.

The next day Jack and I happened to be in the barn saddling up our horses at the same time. I moved Mouse as far from Jack as I could.

"You packed yet?" Jack shouted.

I ignored him.

"You better not wait 'til the last minute!"

I ignored him.

Just as I prepared to head out, he threw out one last thing. "Let me know if you need a hand."

As much as I knew I should keep my mouth shut, I couldn't stop myself. "We're not going anywhere," I shouted, the words spitting from my mouth in an angry tumble.

He laughed.

Chapter 26

One night a month later I sat down to dinner, my jaw tight. Oscar and I had spent the entire day trying to pull the tractor out of the river bed where it had sunk into the gumbo. It was still there.

"Nothing yet?" I had asked Rita this same question for the past thirty days. And the answer had always been the same shake of her head.

We hadn't heard a word from the Army. I'd written several letters. And Mr. Barbury had called them at least four times. They hadn't responded to my letters, and their standard reply to Mr. Barbury was that they would be out soon. They didn't realize that we only had two more months left on the ranch.

I filled my mouth with fried chicken, although I hadn't been able to taste my food for weeks.

"You mind if I head into town a little early Friday?" Oscar asked.

"Depends on if we get that damn tractor out," I said.

Oscar nodded, clearly disappointed. The phone started to jangle, and it was our long-short-long ring. Rita answered, then held the receiver toward me.

"Who is it?" I mouthed.

She covered the receiver. "Steve."

I nodded, getting up from my meal. After Steve and I exchanged greetings, I heard an eavesdropper breathing on the party line.

"What's up, Steve?"

"I got something I want to talk to you guys about, Blake. You have time to come by sometime in the next few days?"

"Sure, Steve. Just tell me when."

"Well, Bob said tomorrow would be best for them. How does that sound?"

My shoulders tensed at the mention of Bob. "Who else is going to be there?"

"Just you folks…the Arbuckles."

"Yeah…sure. Tomorrow evening will be fine."

After Steve hung up I listened for another click, and sure enough, it came a few seconds later.

Rita questioned me with her eyes.

"Steve wants to meet with us…all of us." I indicated the other house with a wave of my hand.

Rita looked worried. "I wonder why."

I shook my head. "Hard to say. Maybe he's going to try and get us all to make up."

Rita chuckled.

The next evening we drove over to the Glasser place. Bob's car was already parked out front. My chest was tight, and entering the house felt like walking into a bar in a strange town. We exchanged looks as if we'd never laid eyes on each other.

Steve fidgeted. Every time I'd seen him since Jenny's death, he looked thinner, as if the grief was taking small bites out of him every day. He sucked on cigarettes as if they would prolong his life. Finally I said, "So what's going on, Steve?"

Steve leaned forward, propping his elbows on his knees. He dropped his eyes. "I can't do this any more."

"What do you mean?" Rita asked.

"I just can't do it…I'm plum worn out…I need to sell the place."

We all sat in a silent effort to comprehend this information, a quiet accompanied only by the steady whir of the Glasser generator.

"What about Margie?" I asked.

"Well, that's why I wanted to talk to you folks. I want to offer up the place to you first. I'd love to be able to turn it over to Margie and Teddy, but they don't have the means…I got nothing to pass on to them except this big ol' chunk of dirt."

I sat there a little stunned, not only by Steve's decision to leave, but by the realization of how little Steve knew about the state of our family. I watched him look around at our blank expressions, and I imagined how confusing this must be. Steve had no way of knowing that he had presented one more complication to our already complicated lives.

"Well, we appreciate you thinking of us first," I said. "We'll have to think it over, of course."

Steve nodded, but he looked like a kid that didn't get what he wanted for Christmas.

"May I ask a question?" The syrup dripped off Helen's voice.

"Of course." Steve turned his body toward her.

"What kind of price were you thinking about?"

"Good lord." Bob ran a hand down his face.

"I'm only asking," Helen said.

"Well, maybe it would be best to wait and discuss that later," I suggested.

"I don't see why we can't discuss it now," Jack said.

"There's no reason to put Steve on the spot," Rita said.

Steve looked more confused than ever. "Is this a bad time?"

"No no no," Jack slapped his thighs with both hands. "No, this is great."

Steve looked helplessly at me, and I could only shrug and drop my eyes.

"Well, I haven't given the price a whole lot of thought," Steve said.

"The market price is around twenty dollars an acre," Helen said.

"Well, that will give us something to start with then," I said, trying to inject some finality into my voice. "So we can sit down and talk about it. We shouldn't keep you, Steve."

Rita stood. "That's right. We should get going."

Bob also started to stand, but Jack and Helen didn't move. I had taken steps for the door, but I had the horrible feeling that leaving Steve alone with Jack and Helen would be like handing his head to them. Rita was ahead of me, and I reached for her arm.

"Is there any information you need from us, Steve?" I asked.

"Thought you were leaving," Jack said.

I shot Jack a look, then turned back to Steve, repeating my question with my eyes.

"I don't think I need anything from you folks…not until I know whether you're interested."

"Oh, we're interested," Jack said.

"Did I miss something?" Rita asked.

Jack turned to her and looked confused for a moment. His expression changed in the time it took him to comprehend my wife's indignation. A big smile bloomed. "Blake, you old dog you. You haven't told your wife, have you?"

"Hasn't told me what?" Rita's eyes snapped, shooting sparks at her ex-husband.

Jack tilted his head toward me. "I think your current husband better be the one to share that information."

"What are you two talking about?" Helen tried to appear innocent, but I could see a fury in her eyes looking at Jack. I was surprised Jack hadn't told her. Jack fixed that big old smile on his face and raised his brows high. "Blake?"

"Let's go, Rita." I took my wife's hand.

"You don't want to tell everyone, Blake?" Jack said to my back, laughing.

I pulled at Rita, much harder than I should have, and even before the door slammed, she said to me, "What on earth is going on?"

Rita and I sat on opposite sides of the bed, our backs to each other. Benjamin slept just a few feet away, his breath soft and even.

"I can't believe you didn't tell me." The hurt in Rita's voice was thick, profound.

"I just didn't think it was worth having both of us worry."

"Blake! Losing our house? Besides, don't you think I've been worried anyway? I knew something was on your mind, for god's sake." She slumped. "I can't believe you didn't tell me."

"I'm sorry."

"What are we going to do?"

"Well, I keep hoping the Army will show up and haul Jack away, but I've got a couple of other ideas."

Rita turned, the hurt still in her eyes. "You do?"
"I think so. I hope so."

Chapter 27

I have never been as exhausted as I was for the next few weeks. The price of abundance is measured in the hours required to sustain that abundance, and our abundance was wearing me down. But this fatigue ran deeper than work. It was more than physical exhaustion. My bones felt hollow, my muscles drained of blood. I felt like a walking shell of skin held together by some distant memory of strength. And more importantly, for the first time I could remember, I had no passion. I woke up every day with the feeling that I was being moved from place to place like a figure in a children's board game.

Before I got married I had often worked on Sundays if I didn't have any social obligations. Because something always needed doing, and sitting around with that thought in the back of my mind had always been like lying on a jagged rock. But since the wedding, Rita usually made a pretty convincing case for relaxing on Sundays. I still felt uncomfortable about it.

During those last few weeks of the fall of 1949, Sundays became my sustenance. Those hours with my wife and child filled me up, like putting gasoline into an empty tank. I would sputter into the afternoon hours of Saturday's tasks, running on fumes, my engine coughing. Sunday became the only day of the week that I got out of bed without pausing, or starting my day with a progression of heavy sighs.

The last Sunday in August, Rita and I sat in our placid family portrait, me reading the latest edition of the *Ekalaka Eagle*, Rita putting the finishing touches on a new shirt she'd sewn for Benjamin. She worked the needle through the material like an expert nurse drawing blood, and the red fabric danced in her hands as if it were somehow working its own way into the shape of a shirt.

"I don't know about you, but all this sitting around has me worn out," I said.

Rita smiled behind her flashing needle and nodded.

Outside, I heard a vehicle pull into our drive. It drove around to the back, and we listened to the rhythm of the idling engine.

"Oscar's back," Rita said.

I nodded.

"I wonder if they're getting crazy with the wedding plans," Rita said

"I bet they don't even talk about it."

Rita shook her head. "You're not nearly as funny as you think you are, Blake Arbuckle."

The back door closed with a firm slap and I watched the familiar, rolling walk of Oscar MacArthur. I waited for a greeting, but instead he turned left and his boots clomped up the stairs.

"That's odd," I said.

"Wedding plans will do that to you," Rita said.

"I think I'll go see if everything's okay."

Rita shrugged but didn't argue.

I tapped Oscar's closed door with my knuckle.

"Come on in." The invitation was not enthusiastic.

I opened the door a crack. "You sure?" I asked.

"Yeah." Oscar sat on his bed with his back to the door, but he turned. He held his glasses in his lap, and he perched them on his nose, locking the wings over his ears.

"You all right?"

Oscar's chin tilted down. He shook his head a little.

"What happened?"

Oscar pulled his mouth to one side. "Georgia's dad heard about my little secret."

I frowned. "So…what did he do?"

"He called off the wedding."

"He did what?"

Oscar didn't respond.

I sighed, and although my body felt that lifeless drain that had become so familiar, something began to stir. A small pump, buried deep under my foundation, began a slow, steady rotation. I stood and started walking, and the pump accelerated, pushing more and more energy, which coursed through me. My face flushed, and my hands clenched. Running down the stairs really kicked the motor into full speed. By the time I reached the ground floor, my veins nearly burst with thick, angry blood. My eyes bulged with every heartbeat. I went straight for the phone, jerked the receiver from its cradle, and started to ring for the operator, to ask to transfer my call to Belle Fourche, when I realized that the last thing I needed right now was for someone to hear me trying to explain to Georgia's father that there's a conspiracy going on at the Arbuckle Ranch. I slammed the receiver into its home, cursing the limitations of our life.

"What is it?" Rita appeared from the living room.

I stomped around for a few strides before sinking into a chair. I told her what happened.

"Oh no." Rita also sat. "Poor Oscar."

I closed my eyes and took a deep breath. "Rita?"

"Yes?"

I opened my eyes and looked directly at her. "I never in my life believed that I would give a moment's thought to killing somebody."

Rita scooted her chair closer to mine. Her jaw moved forward just a little, then settled into that spot like an anchor. "Me too, Blake."

Our eyes locked.

"Is that the plan you were talking about before?" she asked.

I didn't respond. We just stared at each other for a while. Finally, I rubbed my face with both hands. "I can't believe we're talking about this."

"Well, it's just talk."

"Yes." I nodded. "Yes."

"I'm glad we talked about it, though. Maybe it won't be such a scary thought."

"Maybe."

"Blake, I have an idea, too."

"You do?"

We each revealed our ideas, and it turned out we were thinking the same thing. As we talked, our cheeks turned red, and smiles stretched across our faces. The blood that coursed through me had found a new path.

Chapter 28

"How are your hands holdin' up there?"

Oscar dropped his hay hook onto a bale and studied his palm. "Just like leather, sir."

I shook my head. "You're crazy."

"You just don't want to admit that I'm tougher than you."

I laughed. "As if there was ever any doubt."

Directly above us, the Montana sun cast its heat across the prairie like a fishing net, drying the hay that had just been cut in the meadow next to us. We could barely make out the distant figure of Bob on the tractor, the rake behind him, pushing the thick hay into windrows. Around us, bales littered the meadow like children's blocks. Jack wandered through the meadow on the stacker, lowering the wooden teeth and gobbling up the bales. It was our third cut of hay for the year, something that had never happened in my lifetime. It fulfilled a prophecy Dad had made the year before, providing one more reminder of what a feel he had for the land.

Jack chugged toward us, the weight of the bales rocking the stacker. We stood ten feet off the ground, on the fourth layer of bales.

"Does her dad know you're still seeing her?"

Oscar shrugged. "I don't know. I don't want to ask." A slow smile curled his mouth. His glasses were coated with hay dust, and I wondered how he could possibly see. "It really doesn't matter, when you get right down to it. She's twenty-three years old, for god's sake."

"I don't suppose he sees it that way."

Oscar looked out across the meadow. "Yeah, well...you're probably right about that."

"Some people are better than others at watching their kids grow up."

As Jack raised the rack up toward the stack, Oscar peered at me through those dusty lenses. "Blake, I had no idea you were a damn philosopher."

"One more run?" Jack called out from the stacker.

I waved. "I was hoping you'd say that."

"Me too," Oscar said. "I'm hungry."

A half hour later we all sat up to the table at our house, ready to dig into a hearty helping of fried chicken and mashed potatoes. Despite everything that our family was dealing with…all the suspicions and accusations and betrayals, Rita and I had decided to return to honoring the long-standing tradition of sharing a table during certain seasons. Haying, harvest, branding.

Helen brought the potatoes, the beans, and the carrots. Rita cooked the chicken.

"Great dinner," I announced, breaking a long silence.

The opportunity to discuss a risk-free topic loosened tongues, and the food became the center of conversation for the next ten minutes.

"When are you gonna run that horse again?" Oscar asked Jack.

I caught a very subtle annoyance in Jack's expression, but he turned his head away from Oscar. "Won't have time until after harvest," he said.

"If this isn't the best wheat harvest we ever have, I'll eat this table in one sitting," I said.

"No argument here," Jack said, which almost made me laugh, thinking how little he knew about our past.

"We might have to hire some extra hands this year," I said.

"Can we afford that?" Helen asked.

I snorted involuntarily.

"Blake, perhaps you'd like to explain why that's funny," Helen said.

I just shook my head, still smiling. "I honestly don't think I can."

Helen turned her small face toward me, fixing an intent look. "So you don't think I'm capable of comprehending what you have to say?"

I had to close my eyes for a moment, to allow a surge of sarcastic bile to recede. Then I turned to Helen with the sweetest expression I could possibly fake. "That is the furthest thing from my mind, Helen."

"And yet you refuse to explain why you would laugh at what I said?"

"I didn't say anything about refusing. I said I don't think I can do it."

Helen's head turned in a slow, almost mechanical rotation, around the table. Her eyes recorded every hint of doubt, every indication of skepticism. And she said, "Did anyone else find that humorous?"

"Oh please," Rita sighed. "Can we just eat dinner?"

There was a brief silence, except for the click of forks and knives against ceramic.

"I believe I am owed an explanation," Helen said.

Now Jack turned with a look of fascination and laid down his silver. "Helen, would you please just stop?"

A chill floated into the room, and I'm sure I was not the only one waiting for the inevitable cool scolding from Helen. We all knew it was coming.

Except that it never did. I watched her absorb the command, her back stiffening into that familiar righteousness, like a church organ player. And then she allowed it to sink further inside. Jack had picked up his fork again, and ate as if the world never changes.

That evening, I plopped onto the bed, my body drained of energy.

"Blake, what do you think was going on at dinner?" Rita sat next to me, rolling me into her.

My eyes opened. "That was strange, wasn't it?"

"He's got something on her. Otherwise, she would have dressed him down right there."

I nodded. "You're right...I've never seen her take that from anybody...never."

I had to wonder about the source of this power he had over her. Had he threatened to reveal her role in what happened to Dad? Had he helped pay for their cattle, and maintaining them? Whatever it was, it scared hell out of me. If Jack had found a way to tame Helen, we had a lot more to worry about than I realized.

Chapter 29

The wind brushed a hand over the thick golden shafts of wheat, laying them softly to one side, over and over again, like a mother stroking her child's hair. Oscar and I stood in the middle of the swaying stalks, hands on our hips. I bent, wrapped my hand around a stalk, and ran it upward, peeling the grain from its home. And I popped the handful of grain in my mouth, chewing the sweet, plump buds into a soft gum. Oscar did the same.

"Perfect," he said.

"It really is."

As I swallowed the wad of grain, I couldn't help but wonder whether we'd be around to reap the benefits of this harvest. The wheat was about a week away from being ready to cut, and my deadline with Jack was the week after that. We had still not seen hide nor hair of anyone from the Army, nor had Mr. Barbury made any headway in getting information from them.

My body was weary from fatigue and from too many nights without enough sleep. I had come to dread the setting sun because that meant night, when I didn't have anything to keep me distracted from my racing mind. The fear took hold of my throat, closing it off from breath, and squeezed my heart like a lemon. I woke up every few hours, convinced of a heart attack or a stroke. Rita shared the fatigue from trying to figure out ways to ease my anxiety, as if she didn't have enough of her own.

"You gonna see Georgia this weekend?" I asked Oscar.

Oscar nodded but he looked at the ground, burying his hands deep in his pocket. "I don't know, Blake. I keep thinking this dating business is going to make more sense one of these days."

I chuckled, shaking my head. "Yeah…good luck with that."

Oscar grinned through his murky lenses. "You mean it doesn't?"

"Just like everything else, Oscar my friend."

Oscar adopted a hurt expression. "I was counting on you to give me all the answers."

Three o'clock in the morning found me sitting with my right hand tangled in my sparse hair, studying columns of numbers. The more I studied, the more clear it became that the money we needed to accomplish my plan was just barely there. I had not even thought about what we would do if the plan didn't work. Rita had tried to broach the subject several times, but I wouldn't talk about it.

I heard shuffling feet, and my wife's rumpled figure appeared. "Blake." She drew out my name like a complaint.

"I'll be there in a minute."

"Look at you, Blake. You look like a raccoon."

"You always said raccoons are cute."

"Yes, but I don't want to be married to one. Now come to bed."

"In a minute."

"Blake, you're not going to make any money in the middle of the night, no matter how hard you stare at those numbers."

I sighed, but it felt like the air went nowhere, gathering in my chest like tumbleweeds against a fence. But I knew that lying in bed would only mean more worry. Rita finally surrendered, retiring to the bedroom.

"Blake, are you all right?" Oscar swiveled around on his saddle.

His voice startled me. "I'm fine. Why?"

"You looked like you were asleep."

"Just thinking," I lied. We were headed out to the Three Hills Pasture to make one last check on the cattle before harvest. We knew there were a few cows that needed to be brought in for medical attention, so we had to ride. Of course, a day on a horse is like a day in a rocking chair, the worst possible thing for the sleep-deprived. The one thing that kept me awake was the solid purple/gray wall trudging along the eastern sky like a bad memory. With the wheat harvest two days off, this was one of the few times of the year when moisture was not welcome.

"You sure you're okay?" Oscar asked. "Your head is rolling around like a baseball in the back of a wagon."

"I'm fine."

"Well, maybe it will help you stay awake if I ask you a question." Oscar tugged at Patsy's reins until I caught up to him.

"All right. Shoot."

"Listen, Blake…I know I'm not the sharpest pin in the cushion, but something's going on around this place. And you know…I'm gonna have a family soon, if everything goes according to plan."

He stopped long enough to measure me. I nodded.

"So I gotta ask you, Blake…if there's something I should know. I've never had a job I liked this much. But I need to know if I should be sniffing around for other prospects."

In a matter of seconds, my mind, despite moving with the sluggish ooze of fatigue, considered several factors.

"Oscar, you got nothing to worry about," I said, and the words sat like sour milk on my tongue. I was convinced that even if Oscar couldn't see the lie in my face, he must surely hear it in my voice.

But he said, "That's all I want to know" with a definitive nod.

I returned the nod, but turned my head away. Now I was wide awake.

"Seriously, Blake. Something's going on around here. I know it's none of my business, but you've been walking around like you're waiting for a call from the president or something."

I heard Oscar, but over my shoulder the gray wall moved closer, pushing a cool, wet wind in front of it.

"Blake?"

"I'm sorry, Oscar. I'm worried about that storm." I nodded.

"Yeah, I been eyeing that myself."

It only took a few minutes for the cool breeze to grow into a wind that ruffled our hat brims, billowed our clothes, and threw the horses' tails into the air. The gray surrounded us. I could taste the moisture in the air. And it didn't taste like rain.

"We better head back," I said.

"Yeah we should."

We pulled the reins across our horses' necks, and in the time it took us to change direction, the sky descended with purpose. We were two tiny figures inching along a massive gray canvas. I dug my heels into Mouse's flanks and Oscar followed suit with Patsy. The horses smelled the barn and lowered their heads into a gallop. Ten strides later, I felt a pellet against my cheek, and I screamed, shooting words I almost never use, like bullets, into the sky. And just as if there were thousands of marksman hunched among the clouds waiting for the excuse to return fire, the hail came down on us in a sudden flurry. Oscar and I punished our horses' flanks, trying to escape the assault. Patsy bolted far ahead of my older horse, and for a moment I worried about pushing Mouse harder than I should. But the pea-sized hailstones pelted my face with such relentless force that I pounded his flanks.

As I rode, I found myself talking out loud. I realized I was talking to the wheat, telling it to hang on tight to those sturdy stalks, to not let go. I was thinking what a good year we'd had, and trying like hell to convince myself that the good strong quality of our wheat would be able to shrug off this hail as a temporary nuisance, an annoying but harmless pat on the head.

By the time we could see the barn, Patsy and Oscar were fifty yards in front of me. Mouse began to slow, the opposite of her usual pace when we approached the barn. I leaned forward, toward her ear.

"It's okay, buddy. We're almost there."

I watched Oscar struggle with the barn door, and I felt the brim of my hat against my shoulder and realized the hail had ripped it from the crown on one side. Mouse slowed even more, and by the time we got to the barn she moved at little more than a trot, her head bobbing nearly to her knees with the effort.

Oscar stood just inside the barn door. I was amazed to see Patsy unsaddled. Oscar held a bucket of oats for Mouse. I swung down from Mouse's back and just as I hit the ground, Mouse collapsed. I had to jump back to avoid her landing on my foot. But I fell to my knees, and leaned over her head.

"Get up, girl. Come on." I rubbed my hand along her neck. "Come on, Mouse. We gotta get inside." The cold hail pelted my face but my skin had become numb from the constant barrage. I stood and tugged at Mouse's reins. Her head raised up, and she turned a big brown eye toward me, an eye that looked as tired and sorry as I felt. I pulled hard on her reins, but she laid down her head with a resigned sigh. Oscar rushed out and took the reins from my hand. He lowered himself to one knee, next to Mouse's head, and he leaned down close and studied her. The hail bounded off his head. He patted Mouse's neck a couple of times, then stood up, and took me by the arm.

"Come on, Blake." He led me into the barn.

"We need to get out to the meadow," I said.

"Blake." Oscar held me by the upper arms. "What are you talking about?"

"The wheat," I said. "We need to get out there and check on it."

Oscar's eyes narrowed. His lips pursed. "Blake, it's hailing. We can't go anywhere."

"Yeah." I nodded. "Right. Okay."

I stood just inside the doorway. Hailstones that were now the size of marbles piled at my feet. "As soon as it lets up," I said.

"What are we gonna do out there, Blake?"

I looked out across our land, blurred by the streaks of ice. "We just gotta go. We have to see what happened."

Oscar nodded, holding a handful of oats to Patsy, who flipped her lip over the grain and chomped. Ten feet away, my horse lay dead.

I stepped from the car and a layer of icy pellets crunched under my feet. My mind locked hard on the idea that those little kernels of grain had managed to hang onto their source of life. My mind tried not to think about the fact that, if this crop was ruined, we couldn't possibly follow through with our plan to retain the ranch. My mind tried hard not to think about the fact that my horse had just died at my feet. My mind maintained an unreasonable optimism about everything. It worked at it like no other part of my body has ever worked at even the most grueling of jobs.

Oscar and I trudged from the two-rut road, across twenty yards of grass to where the wheat began. From the minute we were close enough to see, I knew my hope had been groundless. Between every row, a casserole of icy pellets and grain littered the ground. The stalks that weren't broken stood naked, with only an occasional stubborn grain clinging by a slender fiber. Many stalks were broken, bowing in apology.

I walked among the ruins, and the reality penetrated all of that hard work my mind had done. An ache poured through me like a slow pool of blood. As I staggered along, and the realization that this could be the last time I walked among these rows, I crumpled as if this knowledge had drained me of all strength. I fell to my knees. Then to my elbows. And I wept.

Rita came and sat beside me on the bed, wrapping her entire upper body around my torso, her head settling comfortably into the crook of my neck.

"You need to make that call, Blake."

I nodded, and my head dropped a little lower with each nod.

The next morning I drove to Belle Fourche, not wanting to risk a single soul eavesdropping on this conversation.

Chapter 30

Driving back from the fields five days later, I was thrilled to see a particular Chevy parked in our driveway. "Thank you."

"What?" Oscar turned to me.

"Did I say that out loud?"

"Yes you did."

"Sorry."

"Well hell, Blake. You don't have to apologize for thanking me."

I ran into the house and made a direct line for the dining room. Stan sat just where I expected him, legs crossed, smoking a cigarette. From the kitchen, I heard Muriel and Rita laughing, and I smelled steak.

"Man, am I glad to see you." I reached for Stan's hand.

He stood and shook. "We would have come sooner, but the mine…you know how it is."

I nodded. "I understand."

We sat, and I could see from Stan's expression that he had entered pure business mode. He lowered his chin. "So is everything in order?"

"Pretty much. A few things we need to get squared away."

Stan nodded once. "Well, I'm glad you finally asked for some help, dammit. Just tell me what I can do."

I went to my desk and pulled out a sheaf of papers, which I spread out in front of him. As we discussed the details, Stan found some problems I never would have noticed.

"Are you guys already talking business?" Muriel came into the room and kissed me on top of the head.

"Time's a wastin'," Stan said.

"Well, I'm sure it can wait until after supper," Rita said.

I was relieved to have a little bit of levity around the house. The air had been so heavy lately that it seemed to catch in our throats.

"So when do you want to plan this little powwow?" Stan asked.

"As soon as possible," I said.

Muriel scooped a spoonful of peas onto her plate, then she leaned toward me. "Blake, why on earth did you wait until the last minute to let us know what was going on here?"

I noticed a quick look from Oscar, and my chin dipped a little. "Muriel, dammit...you know how it is. I didn't want to worry you guys."

"Oh, and you don't think we might have been a little bit worried if you suddenly disappeared from the ranch?"

Now Oscar sat up straight in his chair.

I squirmed. "Listen, I thought I figured out a way to deal with this. I had no way of knowing the sky would open up and spoil everything."

Muriel shook her head. "Blake, one of these days you've got to figure out that keeping secrets from your family..." She shook her head again. "Let me guess...you didn't tell Rita either."

"Eventually he did," Rita offered. "But not until I pried it out of him." Rita worked at wrapping a bib around Benjamin's neck. He kept pulling it off.

I felt Oscar's hot glare on my forehead, and I turned to my food, sawing at my steak.

"What are you gals pickin' on old Blake here for?" Stan asked. "He's just trying to hold things together."

Muriel scoffed. "Oh Stan, of course you're going to say that…you do the same thing."

"And what's that?" Stan asked.

"You wouldn't ask for help if your feet were on fire."

"Ha!" Stan burrowed into his food. "Well, I can't really answer that for sure, but I suspect that you're wrong about that, my dear."

"Speaking of help, would you please help yourself to those potatoes and pass them, Blake?" Rita asked.

I spooned up a heap of mashed potatoes, and just as we started to turn our energy toward the business at hand, the sound of feet stomping on the back stoop echoed through the house. I looked at Rita. "This could be interesting."

I assumed Jack would be alone, but the footsteps told a different story. Jack appeared from the kitchen but Helen followed close behind. Bob trailed by several lengths.

"Evening." Jack saluted.

"Hello, Jack." Stan, gracious as ever.

"What can we do for you?" I asked.

Jack sighed. "Just thought we'd come by and say hello to our baby sister, if that's all right." His small eyes peered out over a sarcastic sneer.

"Good to see you, Jack." Muriel injected a small hint of hope into her greeting.

"So you folks just happened to come by?" Jack asked.

"Just drove down for a few days, yep," Stan said.

"Liar," Jack muttered, stopping behind Stan's chair.

"Excuse me?" Stan twisted around in his chair.

"Why are you here, Stan?" Jack leaned into his face.

I stood. "Jack, maybe we can talk about this later…when we're not in the middle of supper."

Jack held out both hands. "Why put it off?"

"Yes, I believe we should talk now," Helen added.

"What makes you so sure we have anything to talk about?" Rita asked.

"Rita, please." Jack gave her his most exasperated look. "Can you show a little respect for our intelligence?"

"Should I leave?" Oscar asked.

"Yes," Jack said just as I said, "No, this concerns you too, Oscar."

"Personally, I don't believe Mr. MacArthur should be here," Helen said.

"He's staying," I said. "This is my house, and he's staying."

"Funny you should mention that…the house." Jack traced the perimeter in a slow circle. "How do you figure that, Blake? That this is your house."

I took a deep breath. "Well, Jack…it's pretty darn simple. This is where I sleep. This is where my family lives and eats and works and plays cards. This is our home."

Jack stopped, faced me, and tapped his chin thoughtfully. "I see." Then he started walking again, head down, still tapping his chin. "But what about this agreement we made, Blake?" He stopped, facing me again. "I assume you've told everyone here about our little agreement, haven't you?"

My lower jaw tightened up against my teeth, and I could hear them grind. I did not respond.

Jack held his arms wide. "Is there anyone in this room who isn't aware of the agreement Blake and I have?"

I watched Oscar decide not to reveal his ignorance, instead turning to his mashed potatoes.

Jack ducked his head again, walking in deliberate steps. "Okay then…it seems everyone knows the score. And if I'm counting right, Blake, the deadline we agreed on is coming up in a few days, isn't that right?"

This time he did not bother to look at me. I did not respond. A long pause followed, with Jack walking slowly, and I watched my brother relish this opportunity to be in charge. He finally stopped at the end of the table and faced everyone. "So, Blake…do you want to talk more about the house…your house?"

"I think you've made your point, Jack."

"Oh?" Jack raised his brow.

"Wow." Muriel suddenly stood. She started toward the living room but stopped at the doorway. "It's amazing what you miss when you're away for a while. I had no idea you were such a jerk, Jack."

"This is nothing," Rita said.

"Is it really necessary to get ugly?" Stan asked. "Can we at least be a bit civil here?"

Rita shrugged. "That's up to him." She pointed at Jack.

The fact that Jack found this amusing told me a lot. I thought back to the days just after our brother George drowned when a harsh word would push Jack into a funk for hours, or days.

"So what's the plan, Blake? Did you really think it was going to help to bring in reinforcements?" Jack tilted his head to one side.

"I'm afraid I don't know what you're talking about, Jack. Our sister and her husband are here for a visit."

Jack chuckled, covering his eyes with his hand. He shook his head for a moment. Then he stopped laughing and his hand fell. His expression had changed as if he'd been holding a mask in his palm. His eyes had gone flat and looked smaller than ever. His mouth was a straight, narrow line. He walked toward me. "You don't realize how serious this is, do you?" His right hand rose and a finger emerged, pointing toward me like a knife.

"I think you're wrong about that," I said.

"Do you?"

I stood up. "Yes I do. I know what you're capable of."

"Oh?" Jack stopped just a few feet away, his finger still pointing at me. "But you're not scared of me, are you, Blake?" His hand fell to his side. "You're not scared because in your twisted little view of the world, being true and loyal means something. You have the truth on your side, isn't that right?"

"I never said that."

Jack whirled around, stomping away. "You don't have to *say* it, Blake. It's written all over you…your face, your attitude." He pointed at me again, and this time his finger jabbed at me like a cruel accusation.

I stared at my brother, at those flat, small eyes, and tried to imagine what had brought him to this place. "All right, Jack. Let's just say you're right, for the sake of argument. Let's just say I'm guilty of this crime of believing in truth and loyalty." I held up a finger. "I'm not confessing, mind you."

"Ah yes…" Jack sighed. "When all else fails, resort to the old family standard…sarcasm."

"What point are you trying to make here, Jack?"

"Point?" Jack threw up his arms and held them there, palms toward the ceiling. "I don't have a point. But I don't need a point, see, Blake." Jack reached into his back pocket, and pulled out a piece of paper. "I don't need a point, and I don't need truth, or loyalty, because I have this." He held it up. "And because you are a man of your word, Blake…" He shook the paper, holding it out toward me. And I thought back to the day after the storm, when he'd scrawled that statement out in the cab of Bob's car.

"Jack, have you put any thought at all into the implications of this?" Stan turned in his chair, sitting sideways so he could face my brother. "Nobody knows more about this place, or knows this land, better than Blake."

Jack just laughed. "Yeah, this place going to fall apart. Well, Blake, maybe we'll need a hand somewhere down the road."

"Bob has been here just as long as Blake, and he knows a lot more than any of you people give him credit for." Helen's head tottered on her neck, her apple cheeks bright red with indignation.

"Bob knows a lot, it's true," I said. "Nobody has ever said otherwise."

"Like Jack said, you don't have to say it." Helen was shaking so much, she had to brace herself against the table.

"All right, listen…" I sank back into my chair. "There is another solution to this."

Jack stepped toward the group. "No. No there isn't, Blake. Don't you get it? That's not the deal." He shook the paper at me. "This is the deal."

"Just hear him out, Jack." Stan held his palm toward Jack.

"No, I will not hear him out, Stan, and what the hell does any of this have to do with you anyway?"

"This affects everyone in this room, directly or not," Stan said.

"I won't hear him out," Jack insisted.

"I want to hear this." This simple statement brought the whole room to a standstill. Unlike anything that had ever been said in the entire history of our little family. All heads swiveled as if a strong wind had suddenly blown through the room. Bob's face went purple from all the attention. Nobody spoke for a full minute, and he couldn't take it. He turned his back to everyone.

"You god damn coward, Bob," Jack finally muttered.

"You will not talk to my husband that way," Helen insisted.

"Oh yeah, that's your domain. I forgot."

The slap came so fast that it brought a yelp from Jack. Helen's blow caught him completely unprepared. His jaw fell.

"Go ahead, Blake." Rita leaned onto her elbows, and for the first time in weeks, the tired resignation was gone from her eyes. "Tell them what we have in mind."

I put my hands on the table, looking first at Jack, who still held his jaw but quickly dropped his hand.

I took a deep breath. "Okay, well…what we're proposing is this. As you all know, Steve wants to sell. Stan and Muriel have offered to help us buy him out."

"No." Jack stepped forward.

"What?" Rita said.

"That is not acceptable."

"Jack, I think you're fooling yourself about how much control you have over this situation," Stan said.

"Am I?" Jack held up the statement again.

"Yes you are," Stan said.

Jack's jaw dropped an inch. "What are you talking about?"

"We'll get to that," Stan said.

"No, tell me now," Jack said. "This is a signed agreement."

Stan glared at him. "We'll get to it."

Jack's jaw worked against his upper teeth and his nostrils flared. But he stepped away, stuffing our agreement into his back pocket.

"Go on, Blake," Stan said.

"Okay. Well, you remember when you folks suggested a few months ago that you had the votes to ask me to leave the ranch? With Stan and Muriel aboard, and Teddy, the balance has shifted."

"What?" Now Jack jumped forward as if he was going to climb onto the table. "You've got to be kidding."

"You are kidding." Helen asked.

"No, we're not," I said.

"What on earth made you think we'd agree to that?" Jack said.

Rita sat up. "We had this crazy notion that you might think about the ranch for a change, Jack."

"And what if I wanted to buy the Glasser place?" Jack asked. "I could buy it myself."

"And why haven't you?" I had wondered this for some time anyway, ever since we discovered the huge sum of money he had deposited in the ranch account.

Jack took a deep breath through his nose and his jaw flexed.

"He won't sell it to you, will he?" Rita asked.

Jack wouldn't answer, but the violent turn of his head told us.

"How would the ranch be split?" Helen asked.

Jack turned. "You're not thinking about this, are you, Helen?"

"I'm just asking, Jack." Helen's eyes flashed.

"We'd have to discuss that," I explained. "There are a lot of factors we'd have to consider."

"Such as?" Helen asked.

"Well, there's financial contribution, the number of years we've spent here..."

"Oh no...this is not going to happen." Jack took the paper from his back pocket again and threw it down on the table, then quickly reconsidered and picked it up again, clutching it tightly, crumpling it. He pointed at me again. "This man agreed here, in this statement, to leave this ranch. No ifs, ands or buts about it. It's all in writing."

"Jack." Stan lowered his chin, staring at Jack from under his brow. "How long are you going to keep this up?"

"I'll keep it up until you all realize that you're wrong," Jack said. "There's no compromise."

Stan took a deep breath and closed his eyes, burying his fingers into his eyelids. Stan let his hand fall to the table, and his eyes opened slowly. He looked at me, and he nodded. Just once, like his laugh. And he spoke in that firm voice. "Jack, we really didn't want to resort to this, but we have some paperwork ourselves."

Jack's response was very familiar, and I anticipated the next act to be just as predictable. He had that look–the one where everyone had become obstacles. We were there to interfere with his life. For a moment, I suspected the scene would play out just as I thought. I even began to feel hopeful about it. Jack would disappear, and my signed statement would disappear with him. And we would resume the routine. Less worries and less headaches, aside from Helen, of course. But for all her nastiness, Helen was at least predictable, most of the time.

But he did not leave. Behind those tiny eyes I could almost see him stacking the assets on one side of his brain, the debits on the other. He tilted his head to one side, closed his eyes for a moment, and surprised me yet again. He didn't ask what we had. It seemed very unlikely that there was only one possibility, considering his involvement in Dad's death, and the whole situation with the Army, and who knew what else. But he didn't inquire. Instead he looked right at me and asked, "What do you want?" His question added one final layer to my surprise.

"You really want to know?" I asked.

Jack sighed. "I'm willing to listen, let's put it that way."

"Well, that's mighty big of you," Rita said.

"I'm not promising anything," Jack said.

"Oh, really?" Rita opened her mouth in mock horror. "How shocking."

Jack ignored her, keeping his gaze on me.

"You know, Jack is not the only one affected by this little turn," Helen said.

"That's true," Rita said, and her sarcasm took on a darker tone. "We are dealing with co-conspirators."

"I have no idea what you mean by that, but you're wrong," Jack said.

"Ha!" Rita shook her head. "You honestly believe we're that stupid, don't you?"

"What on earth are you talking about?" Helen said.

"I think you know very well what I'm talking about." Rita challenged Helen with her glare.

Helen stood as tall as her tiny self could stretch. "If you're referring to that night with your child, you could not be more wrong."

Rita's mouth fell open for a moment, and then she busted out laughing. "How amazing that you would only remember that about that night."

"What do you mean?" Helen asked.

Rita shook her head and a smile curled one side of her mouth. She leaned forward, putting the weight of her upper torso on one elbow, and her hand jabbed the air, directed at Helen. "We know what you did, Helen."

Helen's eyes narrowed. "Rita, you've never been more wrong."

Rita chuckled, an airy, sad laugh, and Bob's feet shuffled into a softshoe.

"Rita Arbuckle, you have no right," Helen insisted. "You don't know me as well as you think."

"Oh lord, I really wish that was true," Rita said through her laughter.

"What on earth is going on here?" Muriel said.

Although I had confided my suspicions about Dad's death to Stan, I had asked him not to convey them to my sister for fear that she would find it too upsetting. So Oscar and Muriel were the only ones in the room that didn't know. Or so I thought.

"Yeah, what are you guys talking about?" Bob took one tentative step, still dancing his awkward shuffle.

I studied Bob, looking for any hint of insincerity in his face. I should have known better. He honestly didn't know.

"Just ignore them, Bob." Jack leaned against the wall, folding his arms across his chest. "It's just talk. Harmless, desperate talk."

"Jesus, do you people ever say what you mean?" The question burst from Oscar like a cough. "All these insinuations and innuendos? You're killing me."

"It's not really their style," Rita muttered.

"Their?" Jack said. "You are one of us now, Rita. Twice." He held up two fingers.

Rita sneered at him.

"Jack, seriously…" I looked up at him. "Who do you think you're fooling? How would you possibly know what we're talking about if it wasn't true?"

"And speaking of knowing what we're talking about…" Muriel planted a fist on her hip. "Is someone going to fill the rest of us in?"

The silence that followed was long. Painfully long. We fidgeted and remembered that we had food in front of us, although it was long cold. I stabbed a piece of steak and popped it in my mouth.

Finally, in a burst of breathless intensity, as if she was expressing the combined feelings of everyone in the room, Rita said, "We're talking about Dad."

Jack's response was immediate. "What?" He stepped forward.

Rita's eyebrows raised and a frown came to her face. "Oh come on, Jack. Don't even try."

"What are you talking about?" Jack insisted.

Helen moved across the room, inches from my brother, and turned her face up to his. "Jack!"

Muriel stumbled forward, reaching out with one hand for the back of her husband's chair. The hand gripped the curved wooden back, and her knuckles whitened. "What about Dad? What did you do, Jack?"

"I didn't do a thing," Jack said. "I thought you were talking about George."

"Jack!" Helen moved even closer to him, although this didn't seem possible.

"Somebody tell me what you're talking about before I choke it out of you." Muriel turned to Stan. "Do you know, Stan?"

Stan's chin fell forward.

"What did you do, Jack?" Muriel started toward him, but Stan held her back.

And then in a movement so swift and quiet that it went unnoticed for a moment, Bob left the house, sliding through the dining room, past Jack, and out the back door.

"Oh god." Jack grabbed Helen, wrapping his arms around her shoulders. "The son of a bitch stabbed me."

Helen started screaming, a sustained, undulating wail that seemed to be channeled through her from somewhere else. Jack collapsed to his knees as we jumped from our chairs and surrounded him. A steak knife handle protruded from the middle of Jack's belly, just below his ribs. Helen looked at the front of her dress which was smeared with blood. She held her arms away from her, as if they were somehow responsible, and her scream transformed into a loud cry. Oscar raced out of the house, and I knew he had gone to catch Bob.

Jack clenched both fists in his gut and pulled at the knife, but he was too weak to remove it. The blood spilled down the front of his shirt, to his pants, and dripped onto the wooden floor.

Stan shouted into the telephone, trying to get through to the doctor in Capital. But Jack tipped onto his side, his face folded up like a fist. A minute later, he had stopped breathing. Then his eyes opened, looking bigger than I could ever remember.

Chapter 31

I ran a curry comb along the smooth, shining coat of Captain Andy, following the length of his neck with my palm. His tail flipped, throwing a few flies into a swirl.

"It'll be okay," I told him. "They're good people. They'll feed you." Captain Andy nodded his head. Teddy planned to deliver the horse to a buyer in Omaha in a few days, while he and Margie were on their honeymoon. We had discovered that Jack had been trying to sell the horse for months, but that word of the incident in Denver had spread throughout the racing world and nobody would buy him. Now finding a buyer proved easy.

I heard the door swing open, and I assumed somebody had come to remind me to come and get ready.

"Hello?" To my surprise, the voice was unfamiliar.

I ducked out of the stall and saw a man in a suit tiptoeing his way through piles of manure.

"Howdy." I started toward him.

"Are you Blake?"

"Yes I am. What can I do for you?"

The man removed his fedora and reached to shake my hand. "Sorry to bother you. My name's Oliver Stamp. I'm from the Army Investigative Services."

I released his hand and dropped my own. "How did I know?" I shook my head, turning my whole body to one side.

"You know why I'm here then."

I turned, fixing an eye on him. "Did no one back at the house tell you?"

"Tell me what? I was instructed by my supervisor to deal with you. I was told there were problems with some of the other family members."

I took a deep breath, surprised at the level of anger. I shook my head. "Where were you guys six months ago?"

"Well, Mr. Arbuckle, we get approximately six hundred and fifty cases a year that go through our office."

"Yeah?"

Oliver Stamp cleared his throat, and looked around the barn for a moment. "So I take it your brother has disappeared again?"

I thrust my jaw forward. "Well, he's gone. But not in the way you mean." I looked at him sideways. "He's dead."

Mr. Stamp's head dropped. "I'm sorry. I didn't know."

"So I figured."

"I really am sorry."

"Listen, Mr. Stamp. I believe you. But my nephew is getting married in a couple of hours, and I really need to go put on my city duds, if you don't mind."

"Of course. Again, I apologize." He reached to shake hands again, but I did something I don't think I've ever done before. I turned away from him.

Rita gathered the hair on one side of her head, bunching it with the rest, which she then formed into a perfect bun. "So was that guy who I think he was?"

"Who do you think he was?"

Rita started singing 'Over There.'

"You got it." I shook my head. I had watched for any indication that Rita was grieving the death of her ex-husband, but there had been none. I had to wonder if it would come later, after the relief wore off.

I crawled into my suit pants and zipped them up. Rita finished fixing her hair and turned to me. "Blake, what's the matter?"

I sank onto the bed and looked at my wife, frowning. "Do you suppose there's any chance of a few years of peace and quiet around here?"

A slow smile curled Rita's mouth. "No. I really don't."

I nodded. "That's what I was afraid of."

The drive from our ranch to the Little Missouri Lutheran Church is about ten miles. In that little stretch of gravel road, you pass the Glasser place, the Courtney place, the Thomas place, then the Loken place. That's it. That's how big the ranches are. That's how much land we need to keep our livestock fed.

That day, we passed the field where our wheat stalks stood naked and broken. We passed the Three Hills Pasture where Bob's cattle grazed fat and shining against the muted landscape of autumn in Montana. The grass had turned the quiet yellow that comes so predictably every September, so we were surrounded by a blond sea. We passed Steve's hayfields, and I was surprised to see signs of neglect. His fence badly needed repairs, and it was clear that he could have gotten one more cut if he'd had the time. When had I become so absorbed in my own problems?

Rita held Benjamin in a standing position so he could look out the window. He had begun to provide more commentary in recent weeks, and he now seemed quite concerned about something as his pudgy legs flexed and straightened. He shouted and banged his palm against the window.

At that moment, Bob sat in the county jail in Ekalaka where he awaited trial. Helen had left the ranch and gone to stay with her family. But the authorities had opened an investigation to determine her role in my father's death.

So Jack and Helen were both gone. Years of wishes had come true. And it had become more apparent every day since they disappeared that I was probably never going to be as happy about this as I always imagined. The consequences were simply too tragic.

It had been a week since I visited Bob. The sight of his hunched figure sitting alone in that jail cell broke my heart into two neat halves, like an apple. And when his eyes lit up, those halves split into still smaller pieces. Buddy put me in the next cell over, so we'd have a little privacy, 'but you won't be in danger.'

"Whatever you say, Buddy."

"Thanks a lot for coming, Blake." Bob turned around on his mattress and sat as close to the bars as he could get.

I reached through the bars and took his hand. "How you holdin' up?"

"Oh, not too bad. The worst part is how boring it is." He tilted his head toward the office, and I chuckled.

"You probably miss that old tractor, huh?"

"I do." He nodded, looking down at his knees.

We fidgeted for a second. "Well, I'm sorry about how all this worked out, Bob."

Bob pulled his mouth to one side. He shook his head. "I still can't believe…I'm not sure how I could be so foolish, Blake." He looked up at me. "I don't know how I couldn't see what was going on."

I sighed. "Well, I don't suppose you wanted to. Even if you suspected it, in the back of your mind."

Bob dropped his head, looking at his hands. He thought for a while. Finally, he sighed and raised his eyes again. "When Jack came back, of course I figured he was up to something. They didn't make any secret about wanting to take over the ranch, of course. I knew that, although I didn't like the idea."

"You didn't?"

Bob looked annoyed. "Hell no. It didn't make a damn bit of sense."

"I don't suppose you told them that."

Bob smirked, fixing me with a 'what do *you* think?' expression.

"Did they ever even ask your opinion? About anything?"

He gave me the exact same look. It saddened me that Bob showed more expression than I'd seen since he was a kid.

"I'm sorry I didn't come to you," he said.

"Well, what the hell could you have told me if you didn't know what they were up to?"

He shook his head. "I don't know. I just know that there were so many times that I felt like telling you…anything…that something was up. That we needed to be careful."

I rubbed my eyes. "It's okay, Bob. We knew we needed to be careful. But I'm not sure what we could have done."

"We could have chased him off, Blake. We should have. God dammit, I don't know why I didn't."

"It seemed like Jack had something on you guys…or on Helen."

Bob nodded. "It was the money. When we bought those cattle, we really got ourselves in trouble. Helen thought her parents would help us out." He shook his head.

"They wouldn't?"

"Hell, they couldn't! I don't know where in the hell she got the idea they had that kind of money. I tried to tell her…" He shook his head and his hand flew up next to his ear, fluttering there. "Sometimes, she lives in her own little world. You know?" He turned to me, desperate to be understood.

I nodded. "I have noticed that about your wife."

Bob chuckled.

"So tell me, Bob…"

He looked at me from the side, then turned away, and sighed deeply. I could tell from his expression that he knew exactly what I was thinking about, so I just let it sit there, available for him to pick up if he wanted. He stared down at his gray wool blanket. He reached out and started rubbing his hand along the surface of it.

"The night Dad died…" He paused, and his hand stopped moving, the callused palm resting on the wool. "When he called to tell us the baby was crying, Helen acted like we'd just won a new car." He looked up. "She had a little bottle with her, and I asked her about it." Bob shook his head. "She said it was some kind of special oil for the baby's skin. Something she'd been hoping to use someday."

I felt like putting a hand on his shoulder…something.

"When you live with someone like that, Blake…you learn not to ask questions, you know?"

I nodded. Bob wiped the back of his hand under one eye and turned away from me. He took a deep breath and let it out slow. We sat quietly for a while.

"Are you going to be okay in here, Bob?"

He smiled at me. "You know what's crazy, Blake?"

I shook my head.

"I killed a man...I killed my brother, for god's sake. And I wish that hadn't happened. But I haven't felt this free in a long time." He tilted his head to one side. "Don't tell anyone, okay?"

I grinned. "That secret is definitely safe with me."

I had often thought back to a day many years ago when Jack and I climbed partway up a mountain near Bozeman. Jack was energized by the climb. He loved being surrounded by trees, looking down from the vista where we finally stopped to rest. But the whole scene had been very uncomfortable to me. At the time, I thought it was because I felt trapped up there. Because the prairie is more open, you don't feel as confined. And you're not as likely to be blindsided in the open spaces.

I can't say that any more.

But as the gravel provided a steady rhythm against the belly of my car, a sense of calm came over me. Looking out over this land to which I had devoted every day of my life, I saw something perfect, with all of its inconsistencies and stubborn unwillingness to cooperate. Its unpredictability and its ever-shifting shapes. On this particular day, the sky had faded to a soft shade of blue, with a few puffs of gray drifting like lost sheep along the eastern skyline. The whole scene looked beautiful to me. I looked over at my wife, in the new green dress she bought for her son's wedding, and at my son making his proclamations, pointing his chubby finger at the beauty outside. I have come to believe that there are only a few perfect moments in a lifetime, and this was one of mine.

As the locals filled the pews of the Little Missouri Lutheran Church, a proudly smiling Teddy stood next to Pastor Ludke at the altar. Rita and I sat in the front row, her hand resting on top of mine. Benjamin sat in her lap, asking questions in a language he assumed we understood.

When Gertie Snodgras tickled the first few bars of "The Wedding March," Rita immediately broke into quiet tears. Steve led Margie up the aisle, and all heads turned.

The deal to buy the Glasser place was all but done, with only a few small details to iron out. Teddy and Margie would live in the Glasser house, and Oscar and Georgia were going to move into Bob and Helen's house, and help Teddy manage the whole outfit. Rita and I would oversee everything, but I had decided I didn't want to be in charge any more.

On paper, none of this made much sense. We were adding eighteen thousand acres of land, two hundred head of cattle, and another six hundred sheep. We'd put ourselves several thousand dollars in debt for the privilege of working harder than ever. But the math had always been off. When you are a rancher, the odds are never in your favor. Yet somehow things always got done.

Margie approached the altar and I smiled at how much better Steve looked. As if he'd been freed of every burden he'd been carrying since we'd known him. His eyes shone. Margie looked like a goddam angel.

"Dearly beloved," Pastor Ludke began, and after reciting the most basic marriage vows I ever heard, he broke from his usual form and addressed the crowd.

"Ladies and gentlemen, this is a wonderful occasion, as you know. We are enjoying a particularly fruitful time in the history of our little community. It makes events like this even more delightful, because of the hope such unions promise."

Rita grabbed my hand again. I thought about the night before, when we were lying in bed, talking about the wedding.

"Oh my god, Blake. He's still a baby."

"Honey, you were what…sixteen?"

"Yeah…well…that was different."

"Oh yeah? How?"

"I knew exactly what I was getting into."

Do I even have to say that we laughed?

After the kiss, the couple entered the world, and we swallowed them up with congratulations. The we ate. And we danced. And we laughed. And we rejoiced in another beginning. The land around us was as rich as it had ever been. The meadowlarks sent their best wishes in a clear, whistling song. A herd of Herefords chewed silently in the pasture right next to the church, staring their indignation at not being invited. And when the reception began to wind down, Teddy approached me and pulled me to the side.

"What is it?" I asked.

"I just wanted to make sure...what time do we start branding tomorrow?

Acknowledgments

I need to thank Kathy Springmeyer at Farcountry Press (also Sweetgrass Books) for her help in formatting the text, as well as her determination to convince me to publish this book with Sweetgrass.

Allen Morris Jones has now designed three of my covers, and I have been so fortunate to have him as an editor and a business associate, but more importantly as a friend. I love every creative bone in his body.

But this book exists mostly due to a long history of hard-working people who never got any recognition for breaking their backs every day in an absolutely brutal country. George Arbuckle came to Montana in the late 19th Century, and those of us who have been fortunate enough to follow in his footsteps have the opportunities we do because of him. Lee Arbuckle, thank you for carrying on that lineage, that tradition of hard work, that determination to be a force of good in the world. I hope that I have also brought a small measure of that into the world.